Realms Of The Fae 3
The Magic Collector

Realms Of The Fae 3
The Magic Collector

Avril Sabine

Cracked Acorn Productions
Australia

Realms Of The Fae 3: The Magic Collector

Published by

Cracked Acorn Productions

PO Box 1365

Gympie, Queensland 4570

Australia

978-1-925131-91-8 (Kindle)

978-1-925941-24-1 (EPUB)

978-1-925131-92-5 (Print)

Genre: Young Adult Urban Fantasy

For the adventures we've shared.

Summer is meant to look after her brother and keep him out of trouble. That's a little hard to do when they find themselves in the realms of the Fae where she can't keep herself out of trouble. Hunted by a Demi Fae and needing to break a curse, Summer fears she'll never find her way home. The Fae are meant to be stories for children. Not something to fear.

*

This story was written by an Australian author using Australian spelling.

Name Pronunciation

Like many names there is more than one way to pronounce the following ones. These are the pronunciations used in this story.

Lonan (lon-en)

Chenoa (chen-oh-ah)

Skah (scarr)

Taya (tay-ah)

Chapter One

Summer sat on the back seat of the car, her eyes closed, her head tilted back as she listened to her music through ear headphones. The car door was open, but it didn't help. Her entire body felt like it was coated in a layer of sweat and the slight breeze could have come from an oven. Central Queensland wasn't the place to be in summer and just because she was named for the season, didn't mean she liked it. Yet one more reason why they should have left her at home. Right now she could be swimming at Mooloolaba Beach, only a few blocks away from where her family lived. Instead, her mum and stepdad had dragged her along to a family celebration for a great-aunt's eighty-fifth birthday. It wasn't her family. Just because Oliver, her half brother, had to go didn't mean she needed to.

She'd had plans for the coming week. And they

hadn't included a picnic birthday party at some national park, far from anywhere, with no phone or internet coverage. She wanted to text her friends and check for messages. It'd be hours before they returned to civilisation and she found out what she'd missed. Other than the party that had been planned for this evening, and every Saturday in December. It was how they'd decided to celebrate finishing year twelve. Today would be the second party and she was going to miss it. Which was unfair as it had been her idea in the first place.

She was partway through one of her favourite songs when a shadow fell over her and the music stopped abruptly. Opening her eyes, she stared up at her mum who held her phone that had been on the seat beside her. The headphones were now unplugged and Kimberley, her stepdad's sister, stood beside Julie slowly shaking her head, giving her a look that clearly said she was a major disappointment. Both of them blocked the breeze.

"I've been looking for you for ages," Julie said.

Before Summer had a chance to say anything, Kimberley interrupted. "Inconsiderate as ever."

She pressed her lips together, knowing that anything she said would only make things worse. Kimberley had hated her since the first day they'd met. Not straight away. That had only come after she'd offered to let Summer call her aunt. Politely telling Kimberley 'I'm right, thanks' hadn't been a good idea. The woman had looked like someone who'd seen a dead fly in the cup they'd been drinking from. A mix of disbelief and disgust.

"You agreed to watch your brother for part of this weekend. Tim rarely gets to see his family and there are people I haven't met that he wants to introduce me to," Julie said. "And stop sulking. You couldn't have expected us to leave you home alone for a week. You're too young."

She'd turn eighteen on the twenty-eighth of February, less than three months away. More than old enough to look after herself. She kept her lips pressed together, barely managing to hold back the words.

"She should be watching him all the holidays with the money you've spent on her for the next semester of sword training. I don't know why you bother. How many times has she quit activities partway through a semester?" Kimberley asked.

Quitting hadn't been her fault. The activities had changed. Like gymnastics when she was seven. The balance beam hadn't looked that high until she was actually on it. And Scouts when she was twelve. Who would have thought they'd take twelve-year-olds abseiling? The instructor was wrong. It hadn't been a small hill suitable for kids half her age.

"Are you listening?" Julie demanded.

After a glance towards Kimberley, she nodded. Why did she have to stick around making things worse? "Where's Oliver now?"

"My brother-in-law's boys are looking after him," Kimberley said.

Like she could remember who half the people were. "Which ones are they?"

"Grayson and Spencer. I introduced you to them five years ago at the last family celebration you attended." Kimberley's tone made it more than clear that her inability to remember was a major fault.

Why would she remember a couple of boys from when she was twelve? "Where are they now?" Somehow she managed to keep the anger from her voice. She wasn't going to let Kimberley get to her. Not this time.

"Some of the kids went for a walk along the easy walking trail. They'll be back any minute. You can wait at the start of the trail for them," Julie said.

"She should be grounded for making you spend so much time looking for her," Kimberley said.

Leaving the headphones on the seat, Summer got out of the car. It'd probably be best to get started before Kimberley had an entire list of punishments she thought were suitable. "What am I meant to do with him?" She took her phone from her mum and pressed in the plug of the waterproof cover, which hid the headphone jack, before sliding it into a pocket of her shorts.

"It's not that hard to entertain an eight-year-old boy," Kimberley said. "Try using your brain for a change."

Julie sighed heavily. "Just keep him out of trouble, Summer." She brushed strands of black hair away from her face before momentarily lifting up the cascade of messy curls that were tied at the nape of her neck.

Summer bit back the words she wanted to say. They wouldn't help. Only give Kimberley more ammunition. "You could plait your hair, it's a lot cooler." She'd plaited her own messy black curls into a single plait earlier that morning, wondering as she did every summer why she didn't cut it short instead of leaving it waist length.

"Watch your brother. Please, Summer."

Ignoring Kimberley's next complaints, Summer met her mum's dark brown eyes, identical to her own. "I'll look after him." It wasn't like she had much of a choice.

"Thank you." Julie lifted her hair off the nape of her neck again and turned to Kimberley when she continued her complaints.

Seeing the forced smile on her mum's face, Summer felt a touch of sympathy. Not enough though to want to stick around and listen. With a last glance at her mum, she strode towards the start of the easy walking trail. She had no idea why anyone would want to take a walk in this heat. Mid afternoon and she was still sweating. If the previous day was anything to go by, she'd be sweating long after the sun went down.

Spotting a group of kids hanging around the sign for the walking trail, Summer hurried forward, scanning the group for Oliver. As the kids began to disperse, she reached the group, turning in every direction as she tried to find her half brother.

"Something wrong?"

She turned to face a young man who had to be at least six foot. He had broad shoulders, short brown hair that was damp with sweat and blue eyes that seemed vaguely familiar. "I'm looking for my brother. Half brother."

He glanced around before facing a boy that looked similar to him, several inches shorter and his shoulders a little narrower. "Spencer, you seen Oliver?"

Spencer shook his head after a single glance around. "Want me to go back along the track and find him, Grayson?"

"You've lost him?" Could this day get any worse? She was sure Kimberley would figure out some way to blame it on her.

"He can't be too far back." Grayson moved closer to his brother, lowering his voice. "Get the rest of the kids back to their parents and cover for us. Tell them Oliver was tired and couldn't keep up so I walked with him."

Summer had moved close so she could hear what Grayson said. He wasn't going without her. "Tell my mum I went after them." Hopefully that would prevent Kimberley from blaming her for her brother being the last one back. Especially if they could hide the fact he'd been left behind.

Spencer nodded, calling out to the rest of the kids to follow him.

Summer walked beside Grayson as he strode along the narrow trail. "How could you have lost him?"

"Easy. There were nine kids with us."

She wiped at the trickle of sweat that ran down the side of her face. "How far did you walk?"

"We didn't exactly stay on the track."

She grabbed his arm, coming to a stop and tugging so he faced her. "He could be anywhere?"

Grayson shook her hand off. "Of course he isn't just anywhere." He continued along the track.

She hurried after him, dust from the track coating her sneakers. As sweat trickled down her back she thought longingly of the beach. "Who had the crazy idea to run around the bush in this ridiculous heat?"

Grayson glanced towards her with a grin. "You complained about the heat the last time you were here."

She reached his side. "You remember me from last time?" Apart from his eyes seeming familiar, she couldn't recall having met him before. But it was five years ago. He'd probably looked different. She knew she'd changed a bit in the past five years.

"You have to remember I was only thirteen," Grayson said.

It sounded like he was trying to apologise. She tried to think what he could have done. Her mouth dropped open for a couple of seconds. "You tipped the bucket of water on me." It had been balanced on the door of the bedroom she'd shared with her brother.

"I had help. My brother and one of my cousins."

She remembered the water cascading over her. It

hadn't been so bad after the initial shock. At least it had cooled her off on an extremely hot day. She vaguely recalled turning around at the sound of giggling and running footsteps, catching a glimpse of three figures retreating, one of them glancing back over his shoulder. "Why did you do it?"

He shrugged. "You were complaining about the heat and we'd watched a movie about a kid who played a lot of practical jokes on people. It had looked like fun."

"Was it?"

He chuckled. "Until we were grounded for half of the Christmas holidays. My mum also lectured us on how you could have been hurt by the bucket falling on you." He glanced towards her. "You weren't hurt, were you?"

She hadn't been. The bucket had missed her, only dousing her in its contents. But she didn't know if she should tell him. She was tempted to let him suffer a little first. How could he have lost her brother?

"Summer?" He reached for her hand, drawing her to a stop. "Did we hurt you?"

Chapter Two

Summer looked up into Grayson's familiar blue eyes. "I saw you running away. Well, I caught a glimpse of you. Not the other two, only you."

"You didn't say anything. No one knew it was us until we were caught playing another prank and Spencer confessed. Why didn't you say anything?"

What could she have said? *Line them up so I can look into their eyes?* She tried to tug her hand from his. "We have to find Oliver."

His grip tightened. "Did we hurt you?"

She shook her head, tugging her hand away. This time he let go.

"I'm glad. We weren't trying to hurt anyone. That was the last thing we wanted."

She looked ahead along the narrow track, gum trees pressing in on each side. It was a little cooler in their shade, but not by much. "Why haven't we seen Oliver by now?"

"It was a long walk."

She frowned, trying to figure out the tone she could hear in his voice. Uncertainty? No, he was uncomfortable. "What did you do to him?"

"Nothing. He's a little kid. As if we'd do anything to him."

"Then what aren't you telling me?"

"We turn off here." He gestured towards a larger tree, thin layers of bark curling away from the trunk in various places.

"Grayson-"

"We didn't do anything to him. He wanted to come with us. Wanted to hear about the local legends."

She stayed close to Grayson as he wound his way through the trees. How could her brother have found his way back to the path? A glance over her shoulder had her wondering how she was going to find her way back. "What local legends? Do you mean Aboriginal legends?"

"No. Although there are some of them about this area. It was the legends about curses, entrances to another realm and a race you don't want to annoy."

"No wonder Oliver wanted to go with you. That sounds like the kind of story he'd listen to for hours."

"It's not a story. And we're not meant to show outsiders. But Oliver is kind of part of our family. He's the cousin of my cousins." He paused a moment. "So I guess you're kind of family too."

She almost told him that between stepfamilies and in-laws they weren't really family at all, but if thinking there was some sort of family connection convinced him to tell her what was going on, she wasn't about to argue. A cliff face loomed up out of the trees in front of them. Summer turned her back on it, looking in the direction they'd come. Fear rose within her. "Where is he? He could be anywhere."

"There are caves. Well, they're not exactly caves. More like narrow canyons I suppose. He's probably in them. There's a swimming hole."

She looked him up and down. "The day isn't that hot. Your clothes would be wet if you went swimming."

He opened his mouth, closed it, took hold of her hand and drew her forward, following the line of the cliff. "Come on. Not far now."

She should be calling out to her brother, but something about the area made her remain quiet, glad to hold onto Grayson's hand. "I was meant to be watching him." She kept her voice low, barely above a whisper. "They asked me last night. I shouldn't have hid in the car. I should have been watching him." And keeping him out of trouble.

Grayson squeezed her hand. "He'll be okay. Stop worrying about him."

"How do you know?"

Grayson stopped in front of a narrow gap leading through the cliff face. "Because he knows the rules."

Her gaze travelled up, seeing that the gap ran all the way to the top of the cliff. "What rules?"

"Eat nothing, take nothing and whatever you do, don't talk to the Fae." He tried to tug her into the gap.

She pulled away from him, her gaze narrowing. "Is this another one of your practical jokes? What have you done with my brother?"

"I don't play practical jokes anymore. That was years ago." He glanced over his shoulder towards the gap. "Oliver is probably in there. The last time I remember seeing him was after we came out of the waterhole. In the realms of the Fae."

"I'm not going in there. What have you done with my brother? Where is he?" For a moment she thought she saw a hurt look in his expression.

"Wait here. I'll go after him." He turned sideways and stepped into the gap.

A sound behind her had her glancing over her shoulder before returning to stare at Grayson as he moved further into the cliff, the gap widening so he was able to face forward. "You're not leaving me alone." She stepped into the shadowy gap. The smell of dirt surrounded her and a cool breeze brushed over her skin. It didn't make her feel any better. "We should have brought Tim." Her stepdad would have understood. And it would have made her feel better to have an adult with them. The two of them on their own made her think of horror movies where there were no survivors.

"We couldn't. It's the curse of our family. Once we turn twenty-one, we forget all about the legends. That's why we have to pass it along as soon as each of us is old enough to understand. Someone has to know in case the Fae ever decide to leave their realm and make mischief in ours."

"Will you stop with the stories? I'm not an eight-year-old to be sucked into them. If you're setting me up for some big prank, I will get even." She probably owed him for the bucket, even though she hadn't been hurt by it.

"I'll stop for now. But you'll see soon enough."

"All I want to see is my brother. Nothing better have happened to him."

"Summer? Is that you, Summer?"

She froze at the sound of her brother's voice? "Oliver?"

"I'm over here. I got lost, Summer."

Relief rushed through her. Oliver was okay. "Where are you exactly?"

"In a kind of cave."

"I thought you said there were no caves here." She kept moving forward, having lowered her voice so only Grayson could hear.

"Not in this realm. It'll be one of the passageways between the two worlds."

"Will you stop with the stupid stories?" She didn't bother to try and hide the anger in her voice. "Where is my brother?"

Oliver called out before Grayson could speak. "Summer? Where are you?"

"I'm coming, Oliver. I'm not far away." Again she lowered her voice to talk to Grayson. "Where is he?"

"This way. I think."

She followed him through the cliff, relieved when the gap widened and she could walk next to him. On either side of them, they occasionally walked past gaps going off in different directions. Grayson eventually led her along one of the larger passages.

Spotting her brother, she ran towards him. "Oliver."

"I don't know the way out. They said not to use just any path. Only one wasn't cursed." Oliver stood with his arms wrapped around himself, the gap almost meeting in front of him before it widened behind him into an area that would be large enough to be called a cave.

Grayson grabbed hold of her before she could enter the gap separating them from her brother. "Let go of me." She tried to shake him off, but his grip tightened.

"It's a cursed exit. We'll have to go through the natural portal and show him the way out."

She couldn't believe he was trying to tell her the same stupid story. "Let me go." She swung at him, connecting with his shoulder. When his grip loosened, she spun, grabbed hold of Oliver's arm and dragged him through the gap to her side.

Oliver's eyes widened and he shuddered, dropping to the ground as he cried out, clutching his stomach.

"Oliver?" She crouched beside him as he curled up into a ball, moaning from pain. The gap hadn't been that small that it should have hurt him.

"This can't be good." Grayson knelt next to her, reaching for Oliver. Before he could make contact with the younger boy, Oliver seemed to shrink in on himself. The fine blond hair covering his head lightened and became white fur on a small cat that miaowed pitifully.

Summer pressed her hand to her mouth, unable to take her gaze off the cat. This couldn't be happening. It wasn't possible. Somehow it had to be a trick that Grayson was playing on her. "You-"

He grabbed her hand before she could hit him again. "I didn't do this. I was the one who tried to stop you." Letting go, he scooped up Oliver who'd turned to scamper back towards the cave he'd been dragged out of. "We'll have to take him to the realms of the Fae and find someone to break his curse."

"Are you crazy?" She gestured towards the cat. "That isn't my brother. I want my brother. What have you done with him?"

"I'd tell you to wait here, but you'd probably get into more trouble. Come on. We have to use the natural portal. Who knows what going through from this direction would do to us."

She stared after Grayson as he headed back towards the path they'd initially followed into the cliff, carrying the white cat. That wasn't her brother. She had no idea where Oliver was, but she was going to find out. She strode after Grayson, catching up to him and grabbing hold of his arm. "Where is my brother?"

Grayson met her gaze, giving a slight shake of his head. "You saw what happened. You know where he is." He pulled away from her and continued walking.

She watched his back, wanting to run after him and beg him to tell her it was a prank. A shiver ran through her, like she'd been doused in a bucket of cold water. If it was a prank, she had no idea how he'd managed it. When the cat he held looked over his shoulder and miaowed, she hurried after him. That couldn't be Oliver. Coming closer, she stared into hazel eyes. Did cats have hazel eyes? She didn't know, but her brother certainly did. Another shiver ran through her. She was meant to be keeping Oliver out of trouble.

She followed Grayson, the ground sloping slightly upwards, her mind a whirl of confusion and questions. When he stopped ahead of her, she slowed her pace. The passageway widened, the walls angling in so they nearly met overhead, not far above them. Seeing the reason why Grayson had stopped, Summer froze. The path ended abruptly. There was a several metre drop into a waterhole, a circle of light reflecting in the water from the opening above. A wave of light-headedness washed over her and she took a step backwards. All thoughts of her brother momentarily vanished as she fought to remain conscious.

"We need to go through there." He gestured towards the water below, his other hand holding the cat against him.

She scanned the far wall, trying to avoid looking directly down. "It doesn't go anywhere. It's a dead end."

"It's a natural portal to the realms of the Fae, but you have to make sure you dive into the circle of light. Don't surface until you touch the bottom of the waterhole."

There was no way she could jump over the edge, the distance seemed to be growing by the second. As was her light-headedness. She tried to focus on something other than the drop. "The Fae aren't real. They're stories."

"Stories about a race that are real. History books are stories about real events. Just because something is a story, doesn't mean it isn't real."

She closed her eyes, desperately trying to ignore the drop in front of her. It didn't help. Only had her swaying on her feet. Opening her eyes, she tried to focus on Grayson. Her gaze was again drawn to the light reflected on the water below. Her stomach did a slow turn, making her feel queasy. She took a step backwards. "Where is my brother? Where's Oliver?"

The cat miaowed, trying to escape Grayson's grip. He had to use both hands to prevent him from escaping. "It's okay. Wait here and I'll try and fix this. I thought he'd be old enough to keep up. I've been making this journey since I was five. One of my older cousins took a group of us through. I tagged along with him until I was old enough to go on my own."

She slowly shook her head. There was no way that she was going to wait here on her own. The shadows were lengthening and it'd be dark in a few hours.

"You're right. I don't know how long I'll be. Go back and tell everyone you couldn't find me. Time doesn't run the same in the realms of the Fae as it does here. Days might pass there while only minutes go by here. Or it could be the opposite. But it rarely is the opposite." He turned away from her, facing the water.

Chapter Three

Summer couldn't jump over the edge, but she also couldn't find her way back on her own either. There was no path to lead her to the walking track and most of the trees had looked exactly the same as each other. She had to think of a way to convince him not to jump. "He'll drown."

"What?"

"When you dive into the water." She gestured towards the cat. "He'll drown. How can he hold his breath?"

Grayson stared at the cat. "I can't break the curse. Only one of the Fae can. Oliver will have to hold his breath."

The cat miaowed pitifully.

"I don't think he can." She avoided calling the cat by her brother's name. It couldn't be Oliver. Things like curses and the Fae didn't exist.

Grayson looked from the water, to the cat and then to Summer before his gaze returned to the water. "I only have to touch the bottom of the waterhole where the light falls. Anything I'm holding will go with me."

She didn't like the speculative look he was giving her. "I'm not jumping over the edge." She wracked her brain for another excuse. "It's dangerous to dive into unfamiliar waters without checking them first. Anything could be down there. Submerged logs, rocks, anything."

"You don't have to jump. There's a narrow path running down the side." He pointed off to the left of where they'd entered. "It's slippery after rain, but it's been months since we've had any."

Keeping close to the comforting solidness of the wall, she inched forward, spotting the path. It was steep, but not a sheer drop. The path twisted amongst large rocks, which would help hide the bottom once she started down.

"You want your brother back, don't you?"

She met his gaze. Did he know? Was this a prank to force her to admit how much heights terrified her? She hadn't thought anyone knew how terrified she was of heights. Was Oliver part of it? He'd never done anything like this before, but that didn't mean he couldn't be convinced to join in. He'd talked about meeting his cousins for weeks. She shied away from the image of her brother turning into a cat. That had to be a trick. Smoke and mirrors. It couldn't be real.

"Well?"

"Of course I want him back." She took a deep breath. "Lead the way." There was no way she was going first. If there were any traps he could trigger them.

Grayson nodded and headed for the narrow path, stumbling several times, using his empty hand to stop himself from falling. The cat miaowed each time.

She waited until he was several metres away before she followed, keeping her gaze on the ground beneath her feet. If she focused on where she stepped, rather than how steep the path was and how far it was to the bottom, she should be okay. Her stomach did another slow turn and she tried to tell herself she was walking on flat ground. It didn't help. She knew she wasn't.

When Grayson stopped, she nearly ran into him. Looking around she realised they'd reached the bottom of the path. A narrow edge allowed her to stand next to him, the water looking dark and bottomless where it touched the rock they stood on. "How deep is it?"

"Not as deep as it looks."

She eyed him suspiciously. "Are you avoiding answering the question for a reason?"

He held the cat out to her. "Hand him back once I'm in the water."

She grabbed hold of his arm, holding the warm body of the cat against herself. "How deep is it?"

"You'll barely have to go under water. If you hold Oliver above you, he shouldn't have to go under far. If at all. When I get close to the bottom, I'll hold you by the ankle and tug you under far enough so my feet touch the bottom. I'll count to three once I touch your ankle. Give you time to take a breath." Drawing his arm out of her grip, he slipped into the water.

"How am I meant to tread water when you're holding onto my ankle?" The plan was sounding worse by the second. And why was she even thinking about going through with his plan? Oliver obviously wasn't down here.

"Hand me Oliver." Grayson held onto the edge of the rock, his other hand stretched towards her. "I'll give him back to you when we reach the light on the water."

She wanted to argue with him. The cat wasn't Oliver. But he obviously knew where her brother was. "Fine." She'd let him play his practical joke. It looked like it was the only way she'd be able to find her brother. As soon as he had the cat, she slipped into the water, the cold nice after such a hot day. It was lucky she had a waterproof cover for her phone. Something she'd bought due to how much time she spent at the beach and having wrecked two phones because they'd got wet.

Grayson struggled to keep the cat above the water as he swam awkwardly towards the reflection of the light. Ripples from their movement caused the image to ripple and shimmer. Reaching the circle, he tread water, holding the cat out to Summer as she joined him.

She looked up, the curved rock wall seeming a long way from them. No wonder she'd felt light headed when she'd looked over the edge. It was a long way down to the water. "Are you sure it isn't too deep?"

"I've been through the portal hundreds of times."

Deciding to play along, she asked, "Why?"

"What do you mean?" He continued to hold the cat out to her, the creature clinging to his hand, claws out.

"Why would you go through the portal hundreds of times?"

"Because it's like nothing you've ever seen. Not the place, the people. They're amazing. The area this portal leads to is a slum filled with misfits and renegades, but you should see them." He paused a moment. "Take your brother and I'll show you."

The look in his eyes took her back to when she was twelve-years-old and she'd caught a glimpse of him retreating as she stood drenched in water. He'd had the same look, a mixture of excitement, mischief and laughter. Not knowing what else to do, she took the cat, continuing to tread water. The cat dug his claws into her and she tried to disengage them.

"Remember, on the count of three." Grayson sank beneath the surface of the water.

Even with the shaft of light, it was difficult to see him once he'd gone a little below the surface. He went from a distorted figure, to a dark shadow, to an indistinct movement. It made her wonder what else was below the surface. Not wanting to think about it, she looked at the cat. "How can you be Oliver?" She nearly screamed when a hand grabbed her ankle. Taking a deep breath, she held the cat high above her head a second before she was tugged below the surface.

When her hand went below the water, the cat struggled to escape, then she was being pushed upwards, the cat's claws again digging into her skin, a hand remaining on her ankle. Breaking the surface, she gasped for breath, blinking her eyes as she tried to see. The cat miaowed his complaints and the hand on her ankle was joined by one on her leg, the one on her ankle moving to her waist.

Grayson surfaced beside her, his hand remaining on her waist. He used the other one to wipe moisture from his eyes. "Welcome to the realms of the Fae."

She opened her mouth to argue his comment, but she was finally able to see where they were. And it wasn't in the waterhole. They were in a murky river, the side of the riverbank not far from them, darkness making it impossible to see very far. Overhead she could see stars, some of them blotted out by buildings. "This isn't possible."

"Come on. Let's get out of the water. You really don't want to meet any of the creatures who live in it." Grayson took the cat from her, swimming awkwardly towards the side of the riverbank.

She watched as he pulled himself out of the river before she was able to bring herself to begin swimming. It wasn't until she was sitting on the bank, staring at Grayson that it dawned on her. "My brother is a cat."

Grayson grinned. "That's what I've been trying to tell you."

"You did this." She pointed an accusing finger at him.

He shook his head. "I tried to tell you, but you didn't believe me. There's only one exit you can use around that area. All the rest are cursed. The Fae don't want humans wandering in and out of their realms. It also saves them having to guard the entrances."

"This shouldn't be possible." She tried to check out her surroundings, but it was too dark to gain more than an impression of closely packed buildings.

Grayson rose to his feet, holding a shivering Oliver against his chest while holding out his other hand to her. "We need to get warm. It's a lot colder here."

Shock had kept her from noticing she was shivering. Ignoring his hand, she staggered to her feet, wrapping her arms around herself. "We need to fix Oliver. Mum and Tim won't believe a cat is my brother and I can't go home without him." She could imagine what Kimberley would say about that. Even though she hadn't been the one to bring Oliver here in the first place, Kimberley was sure to blame it all on her.

"When you dive into the portal, you come out further down river where a doctor lives. For some reason, when you enter it like we did, it's always up river." He headed along the riverbank, a glance over his shoulder when she remained in place.

A quick look around the area had her hurrying after him. Even though she could see no one, it felt like someone watched her. Or something. "Will the doctor be able to help?"

"I don't know, but he should know what we can do. For a price. Don't trust him. Or anyone. He's human so unlike the Fae, he can lie. But even they can twist the truth without actually lying."

"This feels like a bad dream."

Grayson chuckled. "Not a bad dream. An interesting one." He looked towards her. "I wonder if you'll forget about this place when you turn twenty-one. We can't decide if it's the exit we use or something to do with our family. The portal we used might be a different kind of cursed exit to the other ones. We regularly argue over which is the correct answer."

She had no idea what half his words meant and didn't know if she wanted him to explain them. All she wanted was to get her brother turned into a human again and go home. He might be a pain at times, but he didn't deserve being a cat. No matter how cool an animal cats were.

The further they travelled along the river, the more

light could be seen. Being able to see her surroundings better wasn't at all reassuring. Beneath her feet was an uneven cobblestone road, looking like it had been in need of repair decades ago. The river looked murky and there was the occasional ripple, like something swam past beneath the surface, waiting for the unwary. Summer tried not to think about how long they'd been in the water. It was hard not to with her dripping clothes and her hair hanging in a wet plait down her back causing her to keep shivering.

Many of the buildings seemed randomly thrown together, some looking like they'd tumble down at any minute, others having already collapsed into piles of rubble. There were burnt out skeletons of buildings, littered with rubble and vines creeping over everything. These were worse, making Summer once again think of horror movies. Ones with monsters lurking in the shadows. Why had she watched so many of them over the years? Catching the glitter of eyes in one burnt out building she hurriedly looked away. It didn't help. Safety was nowhere to be found. Not in the alleys and narrow streets she could see leading away from the river and not amongst the huddled figures she caught sight of around campfires set on street corners or in the shadowy doorways of decrepit buildings that had mostly tumbled down.

She moved closer to Grayson. "How much further do we need to go?" She didn't voice the other question that came to mind. How safe was it wandering the streets in the dark? She feared she already knew the answer to that question.

"Not far. See the lantern hanging at the front of that building up the street?"

She looked in the direction Grayson had indicated, spotting the soft glow of a lantern, a candle half burned away. The house was dilapidated, but intact. "Don't they have electricity?"

"They have other things instead."

"Like what?"

"Magic."

Chapter Four

Before Summer could comment, a creature ran out of an alley ahead of them. She barely glanced at the man whose dark skin gleamed in the light of a campfire. Her gaze was drawn to the eight spider legs that scurried along the road, attached to the human body in a similar fashion to the way the legs of a centaur were attached. She grabbed Grayson's arm. "Can't we come back here in the day?"

Another creature came out of the alley, running after the other one. At first Summer thought he wore a feathered cloak until she realised they were wings and a part of his body. His narrow face, although as human as the rest of his body, had a hawk like appearance and his hair seemed feathery instead of looking like strands of hair. He gained on the one he chased, slowly narrowing the distance between them.

"What are they?" Summer's words were barely a breath of air.

"They're Demi Fae. The first one is one of the arachnid people while the one chasing him is a Raptor."

"Get back here. I'll teach you not to go pilfering in other people's pockets." The Raptor was now only several metres from the arachnid.

"A dinosaur?"

Grayson shook his head. "Like a bird of prey."

His explanation didn't help with her confusion. "They're animals?"

"No, they're people."

The Raptor spread his wings, using them to propel himself forward the last few metres, tackling the arachnid to the ground. The arachnid fought to escape and other creatures came forward to watch the show, some cheering each opponent on.

Grayson drew Summer to the side, remaining in the shadows of a building. "We'll wait here until things settle down."

She glanced back the way they'd come, about to suggest they return home. That way was blocked by more strange creatures. For a moment she thought she spotted a human amongst them, tall and slim with unnaturally pale skin. Then she saw his ears. There was a slight point to the tips. It seemed like they were the only humans in the area and she didn't know if that was good or bad.

Her gaze was drawn to the fight, which several others had joined, then to the lantern that seemed an impossible distance away. "We're not going to live long enough to reach the doctor."

Continuing to hold Oliver to his chest, Grayson slipped an arm around her waist and drew her against him. "This is pretty normal around here. Stay out of trouble, don't talk to anyone, don't look them in the eye and we'll be right. And make sure you don't eat anything."

"Why do you keep coming back here?"

"To know the truth."

She frowned, dragging her gaze from the fight. "What truth?"

"That life isn't ordinary. That although I'll forget it and the journals I've kept will seem like stories I've made up, for a little while I'll have known the truth. Know that magic existed and anything is possible." Grayson gestured towards the Raptor who knocked the arachnid to the ground before taking to the sky, his wings helping him escape the others who'd joined the fight. His laughter trailed behind him as he disappeared into the night. "Like that. Being able to fly without the use of any machinery. With the power of your own body. Imagine how amazing that must feel. Being able to stare down at the world like it's small and insignificant with nothing between you and the air and only your own abilities keeping you from plummeting to the ground."

Her stomach slowly turned and she tried not to imagine what he described. "No. I like being exactly who I am. I don't need wings and I certainly don't need spider legs instead of human ones."

Grayson chuckled. "I don't want spider legs, but I wouldn't turn down wings. Providing they didn't come with too many conditions. The Fae are notorious for tying you into contracts that can't be broken and keeping you as a pet. Or at least that's what they call it. That or protégé. It'd be more accurate to say slave."

She tried to read his expression. In the shadows of the building it was impossible, but his tone of voice had been more than enough. "You're not coming back to our world, are you?"

"You won't be going home on your own. I'm going back too."

"No, not this time, one day before your twenty-first birthday. You're going to find a way to remain here. In this crazy world where no one is human and the place looks like it's been through a war."

"This isn't all there is to the realms of the Fae. There are other places. Far more beautiful than anything in our world. The Fringes are the worst of this realm and we're not far from the pit, which is the worst of the worst. Half those that live there are insane from iron sickness."

"I don't think they're the only ones who are insane."

He grinned, his arm momentarily tightening around her. "Don't worry. I'll get you home. You and Oliver." He looked up the road. "It's safe to continue."

She doubted it. Just because the fight had broken up and the participants and spectators had wandered away, it didn't make it safe. "Do many of your family choose to remain here before they forget about it?" She stayed at his side, his arm around her, as they walked along the street. It was warmer pressed against his side. They needed to do something about their wet clothes.

"Not many. Spencer keeps trying to talk me out of it. Said I must be mad if the Fae don't scare me."

She thought of the creatures she'd seen so far. "You're not scared of them? You must be mad."

"Some of them terrify me."

"Then why would you want to live here?"

"There are just as many things in our world that terrify me. Nuclear weapons, terrorists, war. This is no worse. Only unfamiliar."

She fell silent as she tried to make sense of his words. It wasn't until they'd nearly reached the house, with the lantern, that she spoke. "They're things we understand. This place, no one could understand it."

He stopped out the front of the building, taking a step back so he could face her. "I do understand it. I've been studying it most of my life. There are rules, even in this area filled with the worst of the Fae. The rules don't always make sense by our human standards, but they can be understood and do make sense to the Fae." He paused a moment. "If I can figure out a way to live in this world, I'll move here. It'll be a far more interesting one to live in than the human world."

She had no idea what to say. She actually feared that she wanted to agree with him when she saw the look in his eyes. And that was the last thing she should do. Get caught up in this world any more than necessary. "Is it too late to see the doctor?" She gestured towards the closed door.

"If the light is on, he's open for business." He

started to turn away, then faced her again. "Whatever you do, don't ask him about how he ended up here."

"How did he end up here? And is he a real doctor?"

"He's a doctor. Not from our time though. He came here looking for a cure for his daughter. They gave it to him. For a price."

"What was the price?"

"Five years in service to the one who cured the child."

"His years aren't up?" She had other questions, but that seemed like the most logical one to start with.

"Long up."

Well that hadn't helped. "You're not going to make me work for the answers, are you?"

He grinned. "The Fae would."

She pressed a finger against his chest. "You're human." At least she guessed he was. Who knew what going through the portal hundreds of times did to a person.

"When his five years were up, he returned home to find approximately forty years had passed and his daughter was an old woman, his wife dead."

"In five years?"

"Yes."

"How much time has passed while we've been here?" Panic rushed through her. How would she explain a long absence to her family? There was no way they'd believe any of this.

Grayson shrugged. "There have been times when I've returned home only seconds after I've left and I've spent an entire day here. At other times a day has passed while I've been here for a couple of hours. Time doesn't run the same between the realms. Or at a set pace."

"Realms?"

"They often refer to our world as the human realm."

She glanced towards the building with the lantern hanging out the front. "Will he help me?"

"Yes." He remained silent for several seconds. "For a price."

The words made her stomach do a slow turn. It had only ever done that when she'd looked down from a great height. Light-headedness washed over her and she closed her eyes, trying not to panic.

"Summer?"

Opening her eyes, she stared up at him. The lantern light reflected in his blue eyes, changing their colour so he didn't look quite human. She took a step back.

"Summer?"

She looked away from him. "We should see what he wants for his help." She stepped up to the door.

"Are you okay?"

"No." She looked over her shoulder, her gaze resting on Oliver. "And I doubt I will be until my brother is human again and we're out of here."

"I'm sorry. I shouldn't have let go of you. I should have stopped you from taking him through the cursed exit."

She turned so she could face him properly. It took her nearly a minute to speak. "It wasn't your fault." She hadn't listened. No matter how impossible, she should have listened. "Sorry I hit you."

"I should have gone after him alone. I should have known better than to take someone who didn't believe. The Fae are too dangerous. I shouldn't have brought you here either."

She started to suggest they see the doctor, but supposed time wasn't really an issue. It would go as slow or as fast as it wished. "Why did you bring me?"

He opened his mouth as if to speak. Closing it again he shook his head. He held her gaze a moment longer. "I wanted you to believe. You looked at me like I was insane. Didn't believe a single word I said. I didn't want you to think it was another prank." He paused a moment. "I wouldn't do that to you again." He gestured towards the door. "Want to knock?"

She nodded before facing the door. It took her far too long to bring herself to knock. There was only silence on the other side. When it continued to stretch out, she knocked again. It wasn't until she'd knocked a fourth time, about to give up, that the door was flung open by a middle-aged man.

The man's scraggly, reddish-brown hair looked like it had been cut by a knife. His matching beard was flecked with grey and as badly trimmed as his hair, his suit coat looking old fashioned and frayed at the edges. His gaze roamed over them before coming to a stop on Oliver. "Another one." He held the door open wide.

Summer followed Grayson into the house, checking out the room. There was a table in the middle, a bench along one wall filled with drawers and doors and another door led from the room, shadows obscuring where it led. To the right were six large cages, four with different kinds of animals in them, two that were empty. A cat, a bird, a toad and a mouse. She nearly tripped over at the sight of them. What sort of doctor was he?

"What was it before it became a cat?" The doctor

plucked Oliver from Grayson's arms and placed him on the table.

Summer hurried forward, snatching her brother away from him. "What are you doing?"

"Finding out exactly what's looking out from behind those eyes." The doctor waved a hand towards the table, a large sweeping gesture. "If you want my help you'll put the animal back on the table and tell me what it should be."

When she tightened her arms around Oliver, he miaowed in protest. She looked from the doctor to the caged animals at the other end of the room then back to the doctor.

He crossed his arms over his chest, his green eyes narrowing. "If you don't want my help, get out and stop wasting my time. I've other things to do."

Grayson took Oliver from her. "We do want your help." He held Summer's gaze rather than looking at the doctor. "The cat was once an eight-year-old boy and we'd like him to be one again." He faced the doctor. "Can you help us?"

"Put him on the table."

Chapter Five

Summer remained close to the table, clasping her hands together so she didn't grab Oliver again. She nearly grabbed him when the doctor took a small mirror out of one of the drawers and held it in front of Oliver, causing him to hiss, his fur rising and his back arching, his tail fluffing out. "What are you doing to him?"

"He can't see who he is, but others can see his true image reflected back in his eyes. You tell the truth. This was once a boy. A relative of yours judging by the similarities of his features," the doctor said.

Summer nodded. "My brother."

"Then you'll pay my price."

Summer started to say she'd do anything. It was her fault her brother had been cursed.

Grayson spoke first. "That will depend on your

price. Magic has its own laws. Exchanges must be equal. Even between humans."

"Human? I don't know if you could consider me human anymore."

"What are you then?" She had the urge to grab her brother and run. Only the thought of what had happened to Oliver last time she'd grabbed him kept her from following through on the urge.

"That depends on who you ask." He returned the mirror to the drawer.

She rested a hand on Oliver's back when he looked like he might jump off the edge of the table. "What if I ask you? What do you think you are?"

He tilted his head slightly to one side, scratching at his chin through his beard. "It's been centuries since I could remember what it was like to be human. I have no idea what that makes me instead."

She stared at him, wishing she'd never asked in the first place. Centuries? How was that possible?

"Will you meet my price?"

"You haven't told us what it is," Grayson said.

A memory flickered through her mind of asking Tim why he always called the staff of any business, he visited, by their first name and introduced himself. 'To remind them they aren't some faceless staff member and that I'm not a random customer. That we're both humans and deserve to be treated that way.' She held out her hand. "I'm Summer."

The doctor didn't bother glancing at her hand. "Names aren't necessary. And the price will be high. You'll need a lot of magic to change him back and someone able to use it. Someone from this realm. A person who can wield the amount of magic needed can't live in your world filled with iron."

She tried again. "What do I call you?"

"The only names I'm ever called to my face are doctor or the magic collector. I couldn't tell you what ones I'm called behind my back."

"The magic collector? Can you use the magic needed to change him back?"

The doctor shook his head. "I send people to collect magic from those not needing it. I wouldn't be crazy enough to keep it for myself, living in this area. The pinch I have is only enough to allow me to live in this realm and eat the food."

"What ones don't need their magic?" Summer asked.

"The more magic someone has, the more they suffer from iron sickness. I've told them they can come to me and I'll siphon off some of their magic to make it easier to live here, deep in the Fringes between the two worlds. The less magic you have the easier it is to put up with the effects of all the iron that seeps in from the human realm because of how close to it we are here. But they won't give up their magic. They'd rather it kill them."

"What do you want me to do?" She had a feeling she already knew. And it wasn't a good option.

"Take it from them."

She was right. The answer had been as bad as she feared.

"You want us to steal magic?" Grayson asked.

The doctor spread his arms, his hands palm out. "Such a poor choice of words. I prefer to think of it as a community service."

"What happens if they catch us relieving them of their unneeded magic," Grayson asked dryly.

"I suppose that depends on how far gone they are. Some of them can be quite rabid."

She couldn't help thinking about the fight between the arachnid and the Raptor. "Isn't there anything else we could do for you?"

"I'm the magic collector. People come to me for magic. A boost when their power is running low, when they want to improve on what magic they have or to gain magic of their own. Everybody wants magic and it takes a lot of effort to continually meet the demand."

Her voice lowered, not quite sure she wanted him to answer her. "Does it kill them?"

The doctor laughed. "They are dying anyway. From the iron sickness. If anything, you're prolonging their lives. Will you help?"

"How much do we need to collect?" Grayson asked.

She'd nearly agreed before Grayson had interrupted. The doctor could have made her collect magic for years. Tricked her like the Fae had tricked him into leaving his family. "How do we collect it?"

The doctor drew a small glass bottle from a pocket of his suit coat. "Six of these. Five are for me and the sixth is for you. Magic you can use to barter with someone to undo the curse placed on your brother. Next time make sure he leaves by the correct portal. Those who make the same mistake over and over again are expected to gather more bottles each time. Maybe then they'll learn their lesson."

Her gaze remained fixed on the bottle. "How long will it take to fill one?"

The doctor shrugged. "Depends on who you're drawing it from. Some are slow and sluggish. Others the magic oozes out and you have to be careful not to spill it everywhere. That could be a problem for you if you wish to return to your realm. Spill the magic over yourself and it will soak into your body."

"Of course I want to return home." She didn't bother mentioning that Grayson eventually wanted to stay. He could tell the doctor if it was important for him to know. "How do you put the magic into the bottle?"

He took a white crystal from his other pocket. "This has been enchanted so it will draw the magic from the Fae. As long as you have it pressed against the Fae, or Demi Fae, with the bottle on the other side of it, then it will keep working until it runs out of power. Which shouldn't be any time soon. This crystal could fill dozens of bottles, which is why you need to leave your brother here. If you don't return, I'll sell him to one of the Fae looking for a pet. Or a pet for their human pet. When you return the crystal and the filled bottles, I'll return your brother. Then you can find someone to change him back."

She opened her mouth to agree, not really having any choice about it. Her brother needed saving.

"Is there a time limit?" Grayson asked.

"However long it takes. But I'd not take too long if I were you. The longer they're in the animal form that's the most like them, the harder it is to turn them back."

"The animal form most like them?" Summer asked.

The doctor gestured towards the cages. "Why do you think there are different animals? The curse turns people into the animal most like them."

"My brother is like a cat?" She stared down at Oliver. "In what way?"

The doctor shrugged. "You'd know him best. Cats are often curious, playful, adventurous, affectionate towards those they like and caring. The way they bring their humans dead animals is the perfect example of how caring they are."

She supposed each of those traits could easily describe her brother. She looked to Grayson, wondering if now was the time to agree to the terms the doctor had set.

Grayson gave a slight shake of his head before he faced the doctor. "You will look after Oliver and see he has everything he needs while he's in your care. That he'll be safe and you'll only feed him food fit for humans, not Fae or Demi Fae."

"Yes. But if you're expecting more than that, you'll need to collect another bottle of magic."

"We accept," Grayson said.

Summer's stomach did another slow turn and she wanted to grab Oliver and run from the room. She allowed the doctor to take him and put him in an empty cage. Standing at the door, she met Oliver's mournful gaze. "I'm sorry. For everything. You'll be safe here. I'll be back as soon as I have a way to make you human again."

Oliver stared at her, remaining silent.

She had no idea what else to say. "I'll be back soon." She turned her back on him before she could rethink her decision about leaving him behind. He was so little, more so now he was a cat. "I need some bottles and the enchanted crystal."

The doctor placed the objects on the table. "No more than half a bottle from any one Fae. Try and keep it to a quarter of a bottle."

Taking them, she put the crystal and half of the bottles in the pockets of her shorts. There was no room for the rest.

Grayson took them from her. "We'll be back as soon as we can." He led the way from the house, having put the bottles in the pockets of his shorts.

Summer stood beside him, her arms wrapped around herself against the cool of the night. It seemed worse after having been inside. "Where do we go now?" Her gaze was drawn to a campfire, two Fae warming their hands at it. She wished they could dry themselves before the fire, but the thought of her brother left behind in the cage kept her from suggesting that option.

"I guess we find Fae or Demi Fae we can get close to."

She glanced around the area. It was going to be impossible finding anyone in the shadows and she doubted the ones in the light would let them come that close. Although getting close to the Fae sounded like a really bad idea. "A pity we don't have a torch."

"I left my phone in the car since there's never any reception at the national park. Otherwise we could have used the light app on it."

She took out her phone and checked its status. "I have about a third of my power left, but there's no reception so it'll go through it faster than usual."

"Turn it off and keep it for a last resort. You never know when we might need it." Grayson looked in both directions before he turned to the left. "Come on. We'll go deeper into the Fringes."

It didn't seem like a good plan, but not knowing anything about the place, she didn't bother arguing. "What's in this direction?"

"Crowds. We might be able to bump into some Fae and take a little magic from them that way. A few seconds at a time."

A glance around the area showed it remained

nearly deserted. "Crowds? There's no one around here. Where are we going to find crowds in this area?"

"Near the pits."

"Please tell me that place isn't as bad as it sounds."

Grayson reached for her hand, squeezing it lightly and continuing to hold it. "No, it's worse."

"Then why don't we go somewhere else?"

"Because it's the most logical place if we want to get this over and done with fast."

She wanted it over and done with and her brother human again. "What do you think it will do to him? Being a cat."

Grayson grinned. "Hopefully not make him want to chase after mice and leave them on the doorstep for you."

She reluctantly smiled. "I hope not too." She paused a moment. "Will it hurt him?"

Grayson shook his head. "I haven't heard anything you should worry about. Although the ones I've heard stories about, who were under that curse, were only an animal for less than two weeks."

Chapter Six

Summer came to an abrupt stop and faced Grayson, tugging her hand from his. "It might take us two weeks?"

"I hope not."

"How long will it take us?"

"A couple of days. We'll take turns. One can rest while the other collects. Then we can swap. We'll have him back to normal in no time. And home before anyone realises we're gone."

"What happens if we're gone for days? Or weeks."

"I don't know. We'll figure it out once we're out of here." He paused a moment. "What are your earrings made of?"

She touched the small round hoops she sometimes hung various items from such as feathers, beads, pendants or charms. They were currently plain. "Gold."

"Not gold plated? They're solid gold?"

"Solid. Why?"

"The Fae might notice if they're a base metal." He gestured in the direction they'd been heading. "Ready to keep going?"

She nearly blurted out the word 'no'. Pressing her lips together in an effort to keep the word from escaping, she continued to walk. The road remained empty. Further along the river, they turned down one of the narrow streets, winding their way along its twisty path. Ahead she could hear the sounds of a crowd steadily growing louder. When they stepped out of the narrow street and into an open courtyard, Summer stopped.

The area was filled with people haggling, drinking, eating, laughing, gambling, shouting, dancing and brawling. Stalls were scattered around the outside, some little more than rickety tables displaying wares. A handful of shops were open, lanterns hanging at their front doors with signs painted inexpertly and there were various street performers with offsiders that held out hats for coins. The area was warm with the heat of so many bodies, lanterns and flickering campfires. It was a confusion of noise, movement, creatures and people. Although she wasn't certain if any of the people were human.

"Where are we?"

Grayson dragged her to the side, out of the way of two brawling figures. "The courtyard markets. The pits are in that direction. Never go beyond this area. You don't want to fall down the pits." He pointed directly across from them.

"What are they?"

"Deep holes, chasms and pits where the dead or unwanted are dumped, all linked together deep underground."

"Why can't we smell it from here?"

"Magic." Grayson paused a moment. "And stay out of the alleys. They're filled with those who'd kill you for something as simple as looking in their direction."

She stared at a man who was knocked out, his opponent rifling his clothes and pocketing several items. "Worse than here?" Before Grayson could answer, she caught a glimpse of a Fae who stumbled out of an alley to her left, pushing his way through the crowd, headed towards them. He clutched at his side, blood staining his hand and soaking his clothes. "Never mind." She wanted to go home. Grayson was crazy wanting to live here.

The bleeding Fae rushed past them, heading down the street they'd entered the courtyard markets from. Grayson stared after the Fae for a moment before turning to Summer. "Do you want to use the crystal first?"

She shrugged, taking out the crystal and one of the bottles. "How would I do it?"

"Keep the bottle in your palm and the crystal against it. That way as you wander through the crowds all you have to do is brush the crystal against anyone you pass and it should collect a little bit of magic if they have any. Don't stop. Keep moving so if any of them notice their magic being drawn from them they won't know who did it."

She rearranged them in her hand. "It feels awkward. Like I might drop them."

"Walk past me and brush it against my skin. It's important it makes contact with skin. See if you can do it so it isn't noticeable."

It took her several attempts before Grayson said she wasn't overly obvious about it. He gestured towards her pockets. "Give me anything you don't want stolen. You won't be the only one wandering the crowd looking to take something."

"Why would you be less likely to have things taken from you?"

"Because I'll stay over there, away from the crowds." He pointed to a flickering campfire, several

Fae warming themselves at it. "When it's my turn to enter the crowd you can take care of everything."

"Okay." She handed over her phone and the rest of the bottles. "I guess…" She looked towards the crowd, not wanting to join it.

"Keep moving. It's safer to keep moving." Grayson glanced towards the fire before meeting her gaze. "I'll take a turn when you need a break and you can wait by the fire."

She didn't know what would be worse. Pushing her way through a volatile crowd or huddling around a campfire with strangers who didn't look friendly. "Okay." She couldn't resist glancing over her shoulder before she stepped into the crowd. Grayson watched her, smiling reassuringly. She didn't feel in the least bit reassured. She should have known this day would be terrible. It had started with one of Kimberley's snarky comments at breakfast. If anyone had asked her, she would have advised against inviting Kimberley to join them. She'd nearly turned around and headed back to bed when she'd seen the woman. A pity she hadn't.

A dark haired Fae bumped into her and she brushed the crystal against his skin before he moved on. The crystal vibrated slightly in her hand, warming at the contact. She was tempted to check the bottle. Instead, she moved closer to a hunched over woman dressed in little more than rags, her skin smudged with dirt. The smell coming off her wasn't pleasant either.

The crystal remained warm as she lightly pressed it against those in the crowd. A green eyed woman with an owl riding on her shoulder, a man dripping wet with pale skin that appeared slightly green, a woman that reminded her of hewn rock and a man that strode through the crowd, looking in every direction, his hand on the hilt of a sword that hung at his waist. There were a few she avoided, like an arachnid and several wild-eyed Fae that looked like they wouldn't need much of an excuse to attack someone. She didn't want to risk it being her.

She wandered the crowd for what felt like hours, eventually taking a break and letting Grayson collect magic. She huddled by the fire, trying to remain awake as the warmth thawed her. There was no way she wanted to sleep even though her eyes felt heavy. She took out the bottle she'd tried to fill earlier, staring at the shimmery dust in the bottom. It was only a quarter filled. There were uneven layers throughout it, from a layer that looked like fine sand through to one that looked like rich, dark soil. One thing the different layers had in common was they all had a slight shimmer or glittery quality about them.

There had to be a better way to collect magic. She didn't want her brother to remain a cat any longer than necessary. Returning the bottle to her pocket, she glanced around the campfire. No one had been interested in what she was doing. Most of them were asleep, one stared into the flames and one huddled close, shivering.

Another Fae joined the handful around the fire and Summer warily watched him. When he paid no attention to her, she relaxed a little. She even drifted off to sleep a few times while Grayson collected magic, jerking awake each time she realised she slept. Grayson eventually joined her by the fire and she emptied out her pockets, giving him the items to look after while she kept a single bottle and the crystal he handed over. He hadn't managed to collect much more than she had. At this rate, it'd take them weeks.

She wandered through the crowd, looking for a better way to go about it. Moving to the edge of the crowd to avoid another fight, she nearly tripped over a figure sleeping near a stack of barrels. It was a Raptor, his wings spread slightly to drape over him like a cloak. His head rested on one of his arms, his forearm coming up behind his head, the skin exposed. She stared at his eyes, expecting them to open. They stayed closed.

Remaining close to the barrels, she crouched down low and inched her way forward until she could reach the arm. The Raptor reeked of stale alcohol, an empty flagon lying beside him. She pressed the crystal against his flesh and warily watched the still figure. He moved slightly, muttering in his sleep before remaining still once more. Wanting to avoid notice, she lay down on the cobblestones. The chill of the stones would have been far worse if she hadn't had the chance to dry herself at the fire. The crystal hummed beneath her hand and she yawned, trying to keep her eyes open. Every time she blinked it seemed to take longer and longer to open them.

She didn't realise she'd fallen asleep until a roar woke her. She looked up to see the Raptor towered over her, his eyes flashing with anger. A glance at the bottle showed magic had overflowed and pooled in her hand and on the cobblestones.

"What have you done to me?"

The doctor's warning came to mind. She'd taken far more than half a bottle from the Raptor. Not knowing what else to do, she slipped the crystal in her pocket before she grabbed a fistful of the magic left on the cobblestones, a fine golden-red sand that had a slight shimmer to it. "I'm sorry." She didn't dare put the bottle away in case she dropped the grains of magic that were trapped between it and her hand.

"You will be." He drew the sword that hung at his hip.

With both hands full, there was no way she could protect herself, even if she had a weapon. She spun and ran. Dodging through the crowds she headed back towards the campfire where she'd left Grayson. Behind her she heard the shouts of the Raptor accusing her of stealing his magic. Why had she quit Little Athletics when she was younger? It might have been boring, but at least she would have learned how to run faster. Although none of the running they'd done had involved slipping through crowds.

Grayson pushed through the crowd in front of her. "What happened?" He took the bottle from her, putting it in his pocket.

"I fell asleep."

He grabbed her wrist since both hands were now fists in an effort to hold onto the magic that slowly trickled out of them. "This way." He dragged her to the edge of the crowd and into one of the alleys. Firelight flickered at the entrance, a different campfire to the one they'd sat at.

"He's going to kill me, isn't he?" She leaned against the wall near Grayson.

"If he catches you." He took out a bottle and held it so she could tip the magic into it. He eyed the contents once she'd finished. "You took nearly two bottles from him?"

Before she had a chance to answer, the Raptor burst into the alley brandishing his sword. "Who sent you? Taking my magic won't keep me away from her. Chenoa will be with me. Nothing you or her father does will keep us apart."

Summer backed up, Grayson at her side. "I don't even know who you are."

"Lonan. My family might not be part of a clan, but they are powerful. You will regret ever siding against us."

Chapter Seven

Summer frantically tried to think of something she could do. Nothing came to mind other than to stall for time. "I didn't mean to take all your magic. I was only going to take a little." Was it possible to return it? Before she could suggest giving it back, he attacked.

Grayson grabbed her hand, pulling her into an alley that led off the one they were in. "Run!"

She wasn't about to argue. Behind them the pound of footsteps kept pace. Ahead was rubbish and rubble to avoid. It took her a few seconds to realise she could dimly see where she was going. Morning had arrived, a dull grey light filtering down to the twisting alleys they ran through.

"Face me you cowards," Lonan shouted.

Did he think they were stupid? Surely he didn't expect them to face him when they had no weapons.

They slid around another corner and nearly dropped into a hole. She crashed into a wall of the alley, pain exploding through her shoulder as she clung to Grayson's hand.

Lonan threw himself to the side, one foot catching on the edge of the hole so that he sprawled over the cobblestones, his sword skittering across the ground. Staggering to his feet, he cursed the two of them.

Pushing Grayson out of the way, Summer reached the sword mere seconds before Lonan did. She faced him, sword at the ready. It was lighter than the one she used at training, but the balance was better and the grip more comfortable. Lonan froze, warily eyeing her while Grayson remained close to the wall to avoid Lonan and the hole.

"Knowing how to hold a sword doesn't mean you'll be able to use it." Lonan took a step forward.

She held her ground. "What makes you think I don't know how to use it?"

"It's a skill humans rarely have these days." Lonan took one more step towards them.

Seeing Grayson was safely behind her, Summer attacked the Raptor. He jumped out of the way, nearly falling down the hole. "Go back the way you came."

"You think you can beat me?" Lonan demanded.

Summer doubted it, but she wasn't about to let him know that.

"We have the advantage," Grayson said. "You're accustomed to using the power of your wings to help you fight. These alleys are too narrow for you to do that."

"You'll let your guard down eventually," Lonan said.

Grayson laughed. "There are two of us."

"Do you expect me to believe both of you can use a sword?" Lonan's tone was full of disbelief.

Summer didn't blame him. She didn't believe they stood a chance either. "Do you want to take the chance you're wrong?"

"I've been training most of my life with the weapons of this realm," Grayson said.

She was so surprised by Grayson's comment that she nearly turned and looked at him. It had been the last thing she'd expected him to say. Although she supposed it made sense. She met Lonan's gaze. "Do you want to take that chance?"

"You're human," Lonan said. "I will outlast you."

When Grayson tugged on the back of her t-shirt, Summer took several steps backwards. She had no idea what to do and feared Lonan was right. He would outlast them and she doubted he'd let them live. She had to find a way out of this predicament. Oliver was counting on them. When Grayson continued to tug on the back of her t-shirt, Summer continued to slowly retreat. She hoped he had a plan. After all, he was the one who kept saying he knew all about the Fae.

Lonan kept pace with them. "You've got nowhere to go."

She frowned as pain began to rise in her body the further they retreated. Her grip tightened on the sword as she tried to ignore the feeling. Was it something Lonan was doing? She had no idea how Fae magic worked and doubted she'd taken all his magic from him. "If you don't stop moving, I will attack you." If she could put some space between them it might help.

Lonan stopped following. "You can have your distance for now. It won't help. I'll track you down and make you pay for stealing my magic."

"In here."

She glanced over her shoulder in time to see Grayson swing open a grate and climb into a narrow tunnel. Slime dripped from it to land in a half dried puddle between broken cobblestones. A glance in Lonan's direction showed he hadn't moved and she climbed into the tunnel, trying to ignore the pain that had increased enough she felt sick from it.

"Pull the grate shut," Grayson said.

She wrapped a hand around the metal, barely managing not to scream at the pain. Seeing Lonan move towards them, she kept hold of the grate and pulled it shut, not knowing how it was going to keep him from following. Letting go, she breathed hard, checking her hand in the limited light. Other than dirt, it looked the same as always.

"Keep moving. We need to get further away from him," Grayson said.

She wanted to get further away from Lonan so that whatever he was doing to her would stop. Keeping hold of the sword and lying on her stomach, she crawled behind Grayson, the tunnel narrowing a metre in from the entrance. "Where do these lead?" The tunnel darkened as they moved away from the entrance and she tried to see what was ahead, surprised after a few seconds that it wasn't as dark as she'd first thought. She frowned. Why did the tunnels also have the faint smell of strawberries?

"You don't want to know where they go." Grayson took up more room than her, his head brushing the top of the tunnel.

She glanced upwards, seeing the slime coated the

entire tunnel. It was bad enough she was lying in it, at least her head wasn't brushing through it. She tried to check over her shoulder. "Why isn't he following?"

"Too narrow for his wings."

"What if he waits for us at the other end."

"There is no other end."

"What? No exit? He could wait back there for ages."

"I meant that there's more than one exit."

"Oh." Relief rushed through her, quickly followed by worry. "How will we find our way back to the doctor?"

"Let's worry about getting away from Lonan first."

She nearly ran into Grayson's feet. "Why did you stop?"

"I'm trying to get your phone out of my pocket, but the tunnel is a bit tight. If we're lucky there'll be enough charge left to keep the light app running while we're in the tunnels."

She was about to say there was plenty of light, then realised his shoulders probably blocked far more than hers did. "Can you hurry up?" She wanted to get further away from Lonan. The pain had eased off to a slight ache, leaving behind a queasy feeling.

"Okay. Got it." When the area around him lit up, he continued to move forward.

As soon as they were far enough into the tunnels that she could no longer feel any pain, Summer guessed it should be safe to speak. That if Lonan couldn't reach them then he shouldn't be able to hear them. "How does Lonan cause pain?"

"What do you mean?" Grayson slowed down. "Take a right here."

"Before we climbed into the tunnel my entire body was aching. Kind of like someone was trying to set me on fire. And I felt like I wanted to throw up." She followed Grayson into the next tunnel, waiting for him to answer. He didn't. "Grayson?"

"Give me a minute. There's a bit of a drop up here. I'm going to go past it so I can enter it feet first. Stay where you are until I let you know you can move."

She watched him move forward and then back into the hole, the phone gripped between his teeth as he clung to the edge of the hole before dropping to the area below.

"All right, you do the same. It's only a couple of metres drop."

She crawled up to the hole and handed the sword down. "Take this for me. I'd hate to cut myself on the way down."

He grinned, reaching up to take the weapon. "Do

you need me to help or can you get down here on your own?"

She tried to see the ground beneath. It was impossible. The light was too bright and made it hard to see beyond the circle of it. "How far is it? Can't you give me a more exact measurement?"

Grayson was quiet for a moment. "Is something wrong?"

"Why would anything be wrong?" She spoke too quickly, trying not to wince at the tone of her voice.

"Summer, it's not much taller than me."

She looked between the top of his head and the edge of the tunnel she was in. Her stomach slowly turned as she gained a better idea of exactly how far above the ground she was. Grayson was probably a little over a hundred and eighty centimetres. There had to be more than a metre between him and the tunnel she was in. At least three metres to the ground. The height of a single storey house. She closed her eyes, almost feeling herself falling. She hadn't thought it would be that far down. After the confined space of the tunnel they'd crawled through she'd expected it to be some sort of junction taking them less than two metres below. Something she could almost step into.

"Summer?"

She couldn't open her eyes.

"We can't stay in here."

"You said there are other exits." No matter how much she wanted to open them, her eyes remained closed and her stomach slowly somersaulted making her feel queasy again.

"I can't get back up there. You'll either have to join me down here or go on alone."

Neither option sounded good. Why had he told her it was only a bit of a drop? He should have said it was a lot further than that to the ground.

"Why didn't you tell me?"

"Tell you what?"

"That you're afraid of heights."

She wanted to argue his words. It would have been a waste of time. Even an idiot could clearly see what the problem was.

"What do you want to do, Summer?"

"Can't you find something to climb up on?"

"There's nothing."

Tears began to form. Ones of frustration and probably fear. How many times had her stupid fear of heights interfered with her life over the years? She'd lost track. Quitting gymnastics and Scouts were part of a very long list that included team building for basketball where they'd been expected to go across a rope bridge and horse riding when they'd wanted her to learn how to jump. She hadn't realised how far off the ground a horse would take her until the first jump. The jump itself hadn't been so high. The horse had acted like it had been ten times the size and soared over it as if there'd been a mountain rather than a pole twenty centimetres off the ground.

"You're not going to sleep, are you?"

"No." As if that was possible while she was thinking about the drop below.

"Think you can open your eyes and look at me?"

He had to be kidding. How was she meant to look down at him? "No."

"Did you want to find your own way out?"

"No." Fear raced through her and she opened her eyes for a second only to close them again when she spotted her phone on the ground at his feet, the light app clearly showing how far she had to fall.

"What about Oliver?"

It didn't help. No matter how hard she tried to make herself move by reminding herself that her brother needed her, she remained frozen in place.

Chapter Eight

Summer rolled to her side so she wasn't looking into the hole anymore. "You go after him. You've got the bottles of magic. I'll give you the crystal so you can finish filling them." She wriggled around until she was able to take the crystal from her pocket. It hummed in her hand. "I think there's something wrong with it."

"What do you mean?"

"It's still humming." She frowned. She should have felt the crystal through the material of her clothes if it had kept humming. "Or it started up again."

"Drop it down to me."

She put her hand through the hole, keeping her gaze on the slime above her. "Ready?"

"Yeah."

She let go.

"Are you sure it was humming?"

"Of course I'm sure."

There was a lengthy silence before Grayson spoke. "I've tied one of the bottles and the crystal in my shirt and tied it to the hilt of the sword. I'm holding the blade between my palms so don't take it until you're holding on and I let go. You're not the only one who doesn't want to be cut."

She slowly lowered her gaze until she saw the grip of the sword poking through the hole. Wrapping a hand around it, she took a deep breath, trying to keep her hand steady. "Okay. I have it." She felt the full weight of the sword when he let go and drew it up into the tunnel with her. "What am I meant to do with the bottle and crystal?" She unwrapped the shirt.

"Exactly what you've been doing to the Fae."

She stared at the bottle and crystal. "Why?"

"Humour me."

"This is a waste of time. We should be finding another way out of here." One that didn't involve her dropping down a hole and breaking her neck. She pressed the bottle into her palm and the humming crystal against it before holding it to her arm. Eyeing the slime that streaked her skin she thought longingly of the beach. "You never said what these tunnels are."

"They used to be stormwater drains back when this was a new city. They don't work anymore because most of the access hatches no longer close so the tunnels are riddled with holes leading to the chambers and passageways beneath them."

"What are those for?"

"Maintenance. Also to access the pipes carrying the city water supply. But there's even less of them left." Grayson paused a moment. "Anything happening with the crystal?"

She opened her hand so she could see the bottle more clearly. It was no longer empty. Fine golden grains covered the bottom, glittering like mica in sand. The crystal continued to hum and grains kept falling into the bottle. "Oh." The word was a whisper.

"Are you sure there's nothing happening?"

She guessed he must have misheard her, taking her exclamation for a 'no'. "Grayson." She couldn't keep the fear from her voice. "How am I going to go home?"

"Tell me what you see."

It took her two attempts before she could say the word. "Magic." It was greeted by silence and she nearly looked through the hole to see what Grayson was doing. "Say something."

"I'm sorry."

"Why?"

"For getting you into this mess."

For a few seconds she was tempted to let him take all the blame. "You tried to stop me."

"I should have tried harder."

"It's not your fault."

"It's not yours either."

She started to argue, but sighed heavily instead. "I suppose not." It didn't help. But having someone to blame wouldn't have helped either. She continued to watch the grains of magic trickle into the bottle. "What do I do with the crystal?"

"Keep it there. Drain off as much magic as possible. You don't want iron sickness. The less magic you have the less you'll be affected." Again he paused. "What did it feel like when you touched the iron grate?"

She momentarily closed her eyes. "Like I'd put my hand in a fire. I thought it was something Lonan was doing." After a moment, she thought of an idea. "Can I use this magic to get us out of here?"

"No." He almost shouted the word.

"Why not?"

"You don't know how it works. You could cause the tunnels to cave in on us."

She tried to swallow, but it seemed unusually difficult. "I really wish you hadn't said that."

"Don't tell me you're claustrophobic too."

"No, but after that comment I might soon be." She continued to watch the bottle. "How long will this take to fill?"

"Let's hope it doesn't."

"Why not?"

"Because that'd mean you took nearly three bottles of magic from him. Or more."

"I have no idea what that means." She shifted, trying to get comfortable. It was impossible.

"His magic will eventually return to full strength. That much magic will probably take a couple of months, but when it does he will come after us. No matter where we are. Here or in our world."

For a moment she thought she might pass out and was glad she was lying down with how light headed she felt. "What are we going to do?"

"Let's see how much magic is in the bottle first."

They remained silent and Summer tried not to think about the bottle that was slowly filling. She supposed she drifted off to sleep at one stage because Grayson calling her name startled her. "Yeah?"

"How full is the bottle?"

"I'm not sure. It seems to be getting darker in here. How is that possible?"

"You were probably subconsciously using magic to see, before you started removing it from your body. It's a Raptor skill. Not everyone can use magic to see in the dark. Your magic will be like that of the Raptors. Of the air, skies and hunt." Light came through the hole. "Does that help?"

"Yeah." The word came out broken as she stared at the nearly full bottle. "How big of a problem is it if the bottle is full?"

"How full?"

Her mouth opened, but no sounds came out. She let the crystal fall to the floor of the tunnel, staring at the scattering of grains across her palm, no room for them in the bottle.

"Summer?"

"It wouldn't all fit in the bottle." She closed her eyes at the panic she could hear in her voice.

"Summer, you have to come down here. I can help you once you're partly through the hole, but we have to get out of here."

"I can't."

"You have to. He talked about his family being powerful. If they're anything like him, it wasn't a lie. Three bottles of magic is powerful. All it takes to get magic started is a handful. You took more than that."

She forced her eyes open and stared at the shimmery grains in her palm. "What do I do with the magic that didn't fit in the bottle?"

Grayson didn't answer immediately. "Drop it down to me."

"Are you sure?"

"Yes."

She closed her hand over the magic before putting it in the hole.

"Open your hand. I'm ready."

She did as he said, leaving her hand hanging through the hole. "I can't climb down. I'll pass out. I've done that before."

"You won't this time. Hand the sword down and wrap the bottle and crystal back in my shirt and send them down to me."

"You should take them. I want you to save Oliver for me." She bundled everything in his shirt and handed it down to him, careful not to look through the hole. The thought of being left behind made fear race through her and her heart pound loud enough it felt like she could hear it. "Collect the rest of the magic and take Oliver home for me."

Grayson took the items from her. "I'm not leaving you behind."

"You have to." She closed her eyes, not wanting to watch as the light faded from below and left her in the dark.

There was a lengthy silence before Grayson spoke

again. "I'll make a deal with you. If you try and then still can't get down here, I'll help your brother."

"I can't." Even the thought of it made her feel lightheaded. "I'll pass out and fall." They'd tried to make her cross the rope bridge. Her last sight before passing out had been the ground coming rapidly closer. She'd later learned that her foot had got caught in the rope, preventing her from hitting the crash mats a few metres below.

"Ease your legs into the hole. If you can't bring yourself to drop down, then you can pull yourself back into the tunnel."

"I don't-"

"Try. Just try, Summer."

She already knew she couldn't manage to drop through the hole, but if putting her legs in the hole would be enough to convince Grayson she'd tried, then she could probably manage that. The thought of Oliver remaining locked in a cage, forever a cat, helped her crawl past the hole, backing into it as she focused on how the majority of her body remained against the floor of the tunnel. She could do this much at least. Her stomach slowly turned and for a moment she feared she'd be sick.

"A little further."

She clenched her teeth together as she fought against the overwhelming urge to throw up. "I can't."

"A few centimetres more. I'll hold your legs while you do."

It wasn't going to make a difference. She nearly spoke the words, but was worried he might not think she'd tried, so remained silent. He had to go after Oliver. "Okay." She felt his hands wrap around her bare legs mid calf. The warmth made her realise how cold she was. It took her nearly a minute before she could wriggle backwards. From her waist upwards, she remained in the tunnel, the rest of her hung through the hole. Swallowing, she tried not to think about the constant somersaulting of her stomach. "I can't." She started to pull herself up.

"I'm sorry."

Before she could ask him what he was apologising for, he dragged her through the hole. She tried to grab at the floor of the tunnel, screaming as she felt her body sliding backwards. Kicking didn't help. Nor did struggling. Then his arms were around her and her body was pressed against his, her feet on solid ground.

"I'm sorry." He spoke the words against her ear, one arm wrapped around her waist, a hand pressed against the back of her head so she couldn't pull away. "I'm sorry."

Chapter Nine

Summer stopped fighting against Grayson, soaking in the warmth of his body after crawling through the damp tunnel, trying to stop shaking. "Why?"

"Because the only way we could definitely get out is through these chambers. Some of the tunnels are collapsed and you might have been crawling around in them for weeks trying to find a way out through all the dead ends. Going back to where we'd left Lonan wasn't an option."

She remained pressed against him, not wanting to move. Not wanting to see the space she was now in. "I want to go home." The words were barely a whisper.

"Once we've rescued your brother."

"I was meant to be at a party last night. Not wandering around collecting magic." She tried not to think of the magic she'd collected from herself. A shudder went through her.

"There'll be other parties."

She half expected him to finish his comment with 'there is only one Oliver'. He remained silent, his arms tight around her. She clung to him, his solidness helping with the continual sensation of falling. "Where will we get the rest of the magic from?" When he tried to pull away from her, she clung tighter.

"Are you okay?"

She considered lying, but it was obviously pointless with how tightly she held him. "No."

"I'm sorry."

This time she didn't hesitate to lie. "Don't be. I'm not." She frowned, sensing the words were more truthful than she'd realised. Facing Lonan in an effort to escape the tunnels would have been far worse than being dragged through the hole, even if she had nightmares about it.

"Are you sure?"

It took a ridiculous amount of effort to answer him. "It had to be done." Even more effort to release her grip on him. Taking a step back, she kept her gaze on Grayson, wanting him to believe her. "I have to save Oliver. I can't do that stuck in a tunnel." If only she could stop feeling like she was falling. Her feet were on solid ground so she shouldn't feel that way. "Where do we get more magic from?"

"I need you to do something for me first." He picked the phone up off the ground, light shining upwards. "Over here." He shone the light on the ground, moving it until it showed a metal hatch, hinges half hanging off one side where it leaned against a small pile of rubble.

"What do you want me to do?"

"Touch the hatch."

She looked between Grayson and the hatch. "Why?"

"It's made of iron."

She took a step backwards at the memory of touching the grate. "Why would they have iron in a Fae city?"

"Because it belonged to humans first."

"What happened to the humans?"

He shrugged. "All the stories are different. One story says the city was once in the human world, but it slipped through to this realm. The story I believe the most is that they upset the queen of the dark Fae. The Fae have a long memory and will always take their revenge. They're also vindictive and often take slight at the smallest thing. Whatever you do, don't let them know how you feel about heights. Don't even talk about it while you're in this realm. You never know who might be listening and will use it against you."

"I don't like to think about it so I'm not about to go talking about it." She eyed the hatch. "Why don't I feel pain from it like I did with the grate? Just by being nearby."

"You removed a lot of magic from your body and while you were in the tunnel there was a solid barrier between you and the hatch. We need to know if you removed enough of the magic. That's why you have to touch the iron."

She took a step forward, her gaze firmly on the hatch. "Will it hurt?"

"I hope not."

Her gaze was drawn to Grayson. "You hope not?" She couldn't help the rising tone of her voice, not with the memory of the pain and the sensation of her body falling still so strong. "What do you mean you hope not?" She swayed on her feet.

"Are you sure you're okay?" He moved close, taking her arm.

She was tempted to pull away from him. And she would once the ground felt steady. "I'm not about to touch iron."

"If it hurts we need to remove more magic."

"Can't we remove more anyway?"

"Summer–"

"Quit with the patronising tone. Get rid of all the magic you can."

Grayson stepped closer. "You're going to need it. Now touch the iron and let's move on before whoever heard you scream tracks us down."

She moved back, away from the warmth of his body. "What is down here?" A glance around the chamber showed they were alone. The rough stone walls were stained by drips and slime in places, cracks running randomly across the walls, floor and ceiling. There was scattered rubble, nothing higher than her ankles, and a doorway led into darkness.

"Anything could be down here. Please touch the iron, Summer."

She frowned, trying to figure out what the tone of his voice meant. Her eyes widened. "You're scared."

He momentarily closed his eyes, tilting his head back for a second before facing her again. "The chambers intersect with the pits in places."

She opened her mouth to speak, but no words formed. She tried again with the same result. In the end, she shook her head, taking another step away from him. Was he crazy, bringing them down here?

"Summer."

She didn't like the pleading quality of his voice. It made her feel more light headed than she already was. Still unable to speak, she nodded, closing the distance between her and the hatch. Standing next to it made her feel a little uncomfortable, but there was no pain like earlier. It took her almost a minute before she could crouch down and reach out a hand to the hatch. This close she could feel a strange sensation in the palm of her hand. Like she was too close to a flame. It was nothing like the burning of earlier. More a warning not to touch. Taking a deep breath, she touched the tips of her fingers to the hatch, pulling back at the sting.

"Well?"

"Uhm." She reached out again, this time pressing her hand against the metal. It was warm, causing a sting like pins and needles. "It's okay. Kind of."

He drew her to her feet. "Then let's get out of here." He kept hold of her hand.

"Where are we going?"

"To find magic." He paused by the doorway, nodding to the sword leaning against the wall. "Do you want your sword?"

She nearly corrected him. "Yeah, I want my sword." If Lonan wanted it back, he was going to have to take it from her. Wrapping her hand around the hilt, she smiled wryly. Not that it'd be that difficult for him. She doubted she was anywhere near as good as someone who'd probably trained a lot longer than her.

Grayson shone the light into a stone corridor, checking both directions. "Any preference?"

"You're the one who knows this realm."

"It doesn't come with a map."

"Pity." She looked in both directions. "I don't know. You choose."

Grayson went to the left. "Keep an eye out for anything. We don't know what's down here and where the pits intersect with the chambers and corridors."

"Okay." She focused on the ground beneath her feet, not wanting to think of how deep the pits would be. Especially since she was starting to feel a little steadier.

They regularly passed chambers and Grayson checked inside each one. Twice they edged past a break in the ground that led off into the darkness. Summer had faced the intact wall and tried to imagine the area behind her was the same as what she faced. It hadn't worked. Grayson had helped her past those sections.

They reached a chamber with a solid timber door hanging from rusty hinges. Grayson shone the light over the interior, including the ceiling. Everything was intact, even the access hatch for the storm drain.

She followed him further into the chamber. "What are you doing?"

"We need to rest. Both of us. We're not about to find somewhere as safe as this."

She turned to eye the doorway they'd entered. "Safe?"

Grayson placed the phone on the floor so it faced the ceiling. "Yes. Safe." He pushed against the door. It barely moved. "If we can get this closed."

Leaning the sword against the wall, she helped him, surprised when the door inched shut. "Are we going to be able to get this open later?" She stared at the iron ring that hung where a handle was normally found. "How old is this place?"

"I have no idea."

"Which question are you answering?"

Grayson chuckled, sitting down to lean his back against the door. "Both of them?"

"Grayson."

He patted the ground beside him. "We'll worry about it later. Sit down. You look terrible."

"You don't look much better." He was covered in dirt and slime, his clothes torn in places.

"Sit down and rest. If anyone tries to get in here they'll wake us with the door."

"Oliver needs–"

"He needs us rested and able to keep going. I need a sleep and you look wrecked." He stared up at her. "Summer."

Sighing heavily, she sat down. "For a little bit."

"I'm going to turn the light off. We'll need it to find our way out of here."

She nearly grabbed the phone from him, not wanting to sit in a stone chamber in the dark. Not after all she'd seen. She clasped her hands together and closed her eyes before the light went out. It didn't help. The darkness pressed in around her. "This isn't safe." She started to rise.

Grayson pulled her back against him. "Nothing is safe, but in here we'll have a warning if something is coming."

She leaned against him, glad of his arm around her. "Do you think he's okay?"

"The doctor agreed to look after him. People abide by their word in this realm. Often they're bound by it, but those without magic usually keep their word too. Particularly if they regularly deal with those who have magic. The Fae are funny about those who don't keep their word."

"They always keep it?"

"Yes. But you have to be careful of how things are worded. They can be crafty about not promising what you want them to. The same when it comes to how the Fae can't lie. Wording is everything."

She relaxed against him, keeping her eyes closed. "Will we get out of here?" When he didn't answer, she tried again. "Grayson?"

His reply was a mumble, his breathing deepening.

Opening her eyes, she stared into the darkness, trying to see him. The chamber lightened a little and she was able to make out his outline, surprised to find the scent of strawberries in this area too. Panic raced through her and she closed her eyes, trying not to think about what it meant to be able to see in the dark. How was she going to return home? Images of magic, scattered across her palm, filled her mind and she didn't know whether to open her eyes or keep them closed. "We're screwed."

Grayson mumbled again, turning towards her, his other arm going around her body as he sank more heavily against her.

A smile partially formed. "You don't know what you're talking about." She nearly smiled properly when he mumbled again. Turning towards him she wrapped her arms around him, glad she wasn't alone. They would forget this when they turned twenty-one. She would remember it a year longer than Grayson. Then she'd forget every second of being here. Including this moment of being wrapped in Grayson's arms and feeling surprisingly safe. She would turn eighteen on the last day of summer. Which was why her father had given her the name. Three years and two and a half months until all this was gone. Stolen from her. Swallowing past the lump in her throat, she tried to convince herself it was a good thing. The words rang false in her mind.

Grayson's words came to her. He was right. The truth was important. And for now, she knew there was more in the world than most people thought. Opening her eyes, she stared across the room, trying to see the far wall. It came into focus, the scent of strawberries growing stronger. Surely she wouldn't forget it when she had magic of her own. Or would it go too? Disappearing on her twenty-first birthday. There was so much she didn't know. So much she needed to know.

Closing her eyes, she wriggled until she was more comfortable, smiling when Grayson's arms tightened around her. She'd ask him after they'd taken a break.

He was right. Oliver needed them rested and now she'd stopped for a few minutes exhaustion was tugging at her. She rested her hand against Grayson's chest, feeling the comforting beat of his heart beneath her palm as she drifted off to sleep.

Chapter Ten

Summer's sleep was dreamless. It was sensation that dragged her awake. The feeling that she was plummeting endlessly, unable to stop herself from falling. She woke gasping, clutching at Grayson.

"What's wrong?" His words were mumbled, his eyes barely open.

She stared at him, able to clearly see him when the chamber should be in total darkness. She wanted to say 'nothing', but the word wouldn't form. When he reached for the phone, sitting on the floor beside him, she placed her hand on his. "Leave it off. Don't waste the battery."

"Then what's wrong? Why did you jerk awake like that?" He drew his hand out from under hers, reaching blindly for her.

"I felt like I was falling."

His hand grazed her cheek before resting on her shoulder. "I'm sorry."

"It wasn't your fault."

"I was the one who pulled you out of the tunnel."

"It isn't the first time I've had that feeling. Every month or two I'm dragged from sleep feeling like I'm falling." She returned her hand to his chest, the beat of his heart beneath her palm faster than it had been earlier. "Sorry I woke you."

Grayson smiled. "You're apologising to me?"

Hearing the note of surprise in his voice, she grinned. "Yeah, I guess I am."

He slid his hand across her shoulder and up her neck, slowly making his way to her cheek. "I can't see anything in the dark."

"I can." Her words were soft.

He kept his palm against her cheek. "Magic always grows. The longer you live, the more powerful it becomes."

"I won't lose it? Not even when I turn twenty-one?"

"No. It'll be yours for life." He grinned. "And you're always going to be far more powerful than me."

"Do you want more of it? I really don't think I'm going to have much use for it." Not when she returned home. It'd only get in the way and give her iron sickness. She frowned, the words seeming strange in her mind. Like something was wrong with them.

"We shouldn't waste the crystal. The doctor won't be happy with how much we've used it and how little magic we have to show for it. We might need to collect another bottle. Or maybe more."

"I didn't think of that." Rescuing her brother was getting further away.

"Although you should be able to draw magic from your body yourself."

"How?"

"By feeling it and pushing it from your body to pool in your hand. I'd be surprised if you had much left after all you've removed from your body."

Taking her hand from his chest, she stared at her palm, trying to find the magic inside herself. It took her a minute and she ignored Grayson's question about what she was doing as she tried to force the magic from her body and into the palm of her hand. Grains formed, the glitter of mica causing a soft glow.

"You did it."

The chamber became a little dim, the scent of strawberries growing stronger again. "Yes." She couldn't drag her gaze from the magic. "I want to fill the half filled bottle." She drew more magic, watching it increase in her hand.

Grayson took the bottle from his pocket, uncorked it and held it out. "You'll have to do it. I can't see in the dark."

She took the bottle from him and tipped the magic into it, watching as the bottle filled. The light in the chamber continued to grow dim until she could only see nearby. "Hold out your hand." She tipped the last few grains into his hand then took the cork from him. "Four bottles filled. We'll fill the other two before we return to the doctor."

"We could take these ones to him first. You can check on your brother. It also might be worth negotiating how many other bottles he wants filled in exchange for the extra power you used up in the crystal."

She froze. "We can see Oliver?"

"I don't know exactly how it works, but he can't keep us out when we need to renegotiate things."

She got to her feet, tucking the bottle into her pocket. "Come on. Let's get out of here." The doctor had better have been looking after Oliver like he'd promised. She tugged on the door. It barely budged. She tugged harder the iron of the ring making her fingers sting.

"Let me help." Grayson turned on the light app and left the phone on the floor, pointed at the ceiling.

"We shouldn't have closed it."

Grayson slid his hand into the ring next to hers. It was a tight fit. "It wasn't safe to leave it open."

She pulled again, focusing all her energy on making the door move. It swung inwards, a gust of air rushing in, the scent of strawberries washing over them. She stumbled, nearly falling at the sudden movement.

"Why didn't you use your magic to start with?"

"What?" She drew her hand from the ring, staring at Grayson who was picking up the phone.

"The air that helped push the door open." He gestured towards the door. "Why didn't you use that to start with?"

"That was magic?" Surely he was joking.

Grayson chuckled. "Did you expect to pull rabbits out of a hat?"

"No, but..." She'd had no idea what she'd expected. "Air?"

"You took magic from a Raptor. I told you it's of the air, skies and hunt. What did you expect?"

"Absolutely nothing. How can I use something when I have no idea how it works? Anyway, I thought if I used it I might make things collapse."

Grayson shrugged. "I don't know."

"Aren't you meant to be an expert?"

"That doesn't mean I know everything." He looked down when his stomach rumbled. "Come on. Let's get out of here and see if we can find something to eat."

"Didn't you tell me to eat nothing?" Her stomach felt like it pressed against her spine.

"That doesn't matter now. Fae magic will make it possible for us to eat what we want without it being a problem."

"But we'll have other problems instead."

Grayson nodded.

"How will we know if we've got iron sickness?"

"You'll know." He shone the light into the corridor, checking both directions. "Come on."

She walked silently beside him, frequently looking over her shoulder. The corridor remained empty as they reached another chamber. She stood behind Grayson as he peered inside, trying to see past him. It was empty. They moved on, not stopping until they reached the next chamber. Her gaze was drawn to a tumble of rags in one corner.

Grayson turned the light off, stepping out of the doorway.

"What-"

"Shh." He reached for her, his hand finding her chin before moving to cover her mouth. "They're alone. Did you want to try and get close and take magic from them?"

She turned her head to shift his hand. "I didn't see anyone."

"The bundle of rags." He took out an empty bottle and the crystal.

"That was a person? I mean, a Fae."

"Yes." He held out the bottle and crystal. "You'll have to be the one to do it. I can't see in the dark."

She nearly told him she barely could see now. "Okay." Placing the sword in Grayson's hand she took the items, slipping the crystal into her pocket until she needed it. The humming when it was in contact with her fingers was unnerving. It took her a moment before she could bring herself to enter the chamber and nearly twice that amount of time to cross the room to crouch beside the bundle of rags. They remained motionless. She saw what might be limbs visible in various locations throughout the torn and dirty rags. How could this be one of the Fae?

She took a deep breath, regretting it instantly. Pressing her hand against her mouth, she tried not to gag on the smell coming from the rags. Not that she smelled any better after climbing through slime all morning. A sound behind her had her glancing towards the doorway. The shadowy figure of Grayson remained there.

Taking the crystal from her pocket, she pressed it against the bottle in her hand and held the crystal against a dirty limb. The Fae shifted and she moved with the limb, realising it was a leg. Magic trickled into the bottle, a rich loamy substance with a faint glitter scattered through it.

The Fae shifted again, half sitting up to stare at Summer. Her face was as dirty as the rest of her, long hair tangled, leaves and twigs caught in it. "You came."

Summer had no idea what to say. She continued to hold the crystal against the Fae, not wanting to draw attention to what she was doing, wishing the bottle would hurry and fill. The scent of strawberries again came to her, making her stomach rumble.

"I knew you'd come. You told me this is where I'd end up if I went against you." Bony fingers reached out to dig into Summer's shoulder.

"I'm not-"

"Give her back to me. I beg you. Give her back." The fingers bit in deeper.

"I don't know what you're talking about."

"She's mine. You can't keep her. I brought her into

this realm. Raised her like my own. Give her back to me."

"Brought her in?" Summer tried to make sense of the ramblings. "A human?"

"My pet. A sweet little thing with the voice of sunshine. You tricked me. She isn't yours. Give her back."

"You stole a human."

"I rescued her from a life that wasn't good enough for her. She wanted to come with me. And I gave her the perfect life until you forced us to flee to the Fringes. Give her back. I came to the pits like you said." The Fae gestured towards the doorway. "They're only a few steps away. Now give her back."

Chapter Eleven

Summer had no idea what to do. Looking into the Fae's eyes she could see nothing sane. She wanted to run. Wanted to pull away from the bony grip and run. But Oliver was waiting for her in a cage, trapped in the form of a cat. "What is her name?"

"You've taken so many you don't know her name?"

"Tell it to me." The crystal continued to hum, but she didn't dare look and see how much magic it had taken from the Fae.

"My little Nightingale. Gale has a voice to rival her namesake."

Summer continued to stare into the Fae's eyes. The wildness in them seemed to be fading. Was it the memories of the human child that was helping? "You shouldn't keep humans as pets."

"You would say that? You? How many do you have? A dozen? More?"

"I'm not who you think I am." She kept the crystal pressed against the Fae's leg, even when she moved.

"Then who are you? Why are you here? What do you want with me? Did he send you?"

"You ask a lot of questions." She didn't want to answer a single one of them.

"I need a lot of answers." The grip relaxed. "You're human. Are you one of his pets?"

"How long have you been in the Fringes?" If she could distract her a little longer she might manage to get half a bottle filled.

The Fae shrugged. "Who would know? After a while time seemed meaningless." She tilted her head slightly to the side. "What is it about you that makes me think clearer?"

Grayson turned on the light app before he entered the chamber. "You're suffering iron sickness."

"Who are you?" The Fae drew back.

Summer moved with her, still not daring to check the contents of the bottle.

Grayson moved a little closer before he sat on the ground, resting the sword beside him. "Your magic is killing you."

"Without magic I'd die in this place. Anyone could

beat me in a fight. I wouldn't be able to protect myself."

"You can't protect yourself in the condition you're in. Deep in the Fringes isn't a place where those with a lot of magic can stay. Not for long." Grayson moved forward, shifting the sword along with him.

"Stay back." The Fae was pressed against the wall. "I don't trust you."

Summer again moved with her, risking a glance at the bottle. Her gaze was drawn back, her mouth dropping open at the sight of the nearly filled bottle. "I'm sorry." She hadn't meant to take so much. Taking it away from the Fae, she noticed the last few grains fill the bottle.

"You stole from me?" The Fae reached for the bottle.

Grayson took it first. "We're saving your life. Didn't you say you're thinking clearer now?"

"That's mine. Give it back. I can't lose my magic too. I need it to take Gale back."

"Does she want to be taken back?" Grayson asked.

The Fae stared at him. "Why would she wish to stay with him? She chose to go into hiding with me."

Grayson shrugged. "Circumstances change. People change. Why not ask her if she wishes to be rescued? And why would you look for her down here?"

"I don't know." The Fae looked around the chamber. "He wouldn't bring her here. He would never come here himself."

"It's the iron sickness. You can't think clearly while you have it," Grayson said.

The Fae grabbed both of Summer's shoulders. "Take more. Another half a bottle. Leave me with a quarter of my magic. Help me think again. I need to get her back."

Summer nodded, wishing she could help the Fae. But she had her own human to rescue. Pulling away from the Fae, she took the last bottle from Grayson and pressed the crystal against it before holding it to the Fae's leg. "I hope you find Gale."

The Fae ran bony fingers across Summer's cheek, stopping at the side of her eye. "You feel sorry for me?"

She shook her head, the fingers remaining pressed against her face. "No. I empathise with you. I have a brother I need to save. He's been turned into a cat from a cursed exit."

"Summer, the bottle is half full."

At Grayson's words, she drew the crystal away. "Why is it filling so fast?"

"I think you're helping it. That slight smell of sweet berries is your magic being used."

"It's strawberries." At least now she knew why she smelt them at odd times.

"Would you take a message somewhere for me?" the Fae asked.

"I wish we could, but I have to save my brother."

"If I made him human again, would you take a message somewhere for me?"

"That would depend on where you wanted it taken, how dangerous it would be to take it there and what else you expected of us," Grayson said.

The Fae grinned. "You have had dealings with the Fae before."

Grayson returned her grin. "You could say that."

"He would notice me. His people know who to look for. But no one knows either of you. I could show you how to use your bit of magic to travel to somewhere close then return to me again."

"We need to discuss it." Grayson rose to his feet, taking the sword with him and holding out a hand to Summer.

She took it, walking with him to the corridor. "Is it safe?"

Grayson chuckled.

She nearly rolled her eyes. "I know nothing about this realm is safe, but can we do it without ending up with more problems?"

"I think so. It'd be good to learn how to use our magic."

"Is that the only reason you're agreeing?"

"We need to break the curse and get Oliver back home. Having a bottle of magic isn't a guarantee someone will accept the trade."

She looked back towards the Fae, now standing and staring in their direction. "Okay. Negotiate it for us."

He kept hold of her hand, returning to the Fae. "What is your name?"

"Taya."

"We'll take a message to Gale and bring back a reply, if you show us how to use our magic to go there and back. You'll need to break the curse on Summer's brother, Oliver, so he becomes human again and allow us to return him home before we deliver your message. We'll need a change of clothes that's more suited to this realm and you'll have to provide us with a meal."

"You're trying to get more out of the bargain than you deserve."

"What part of it do you think we don't deserve?" Grayson asked.

"I shouldn't have to clothe you."

"How else are we meant to visit Gale undetected? We'd stand out in these clothes."

Taya's eyes narrowed and she straightened her shoulders. "I have little in the way of resources. Unlike the one who stole my Gale from me."

"It doesn't have to be anything fancy. Something to help us blend in. It also doesn't need to be new."

Summer was tempted to take a step back when Taya scrutinised her. "Don't get me a dress." A dress would have made it impossible to do half of what she'd done in this realm.

"You can have some of Gale's old clothes. You are both about the same size." Taya turned to Grayson. "You will have to make do with whatever I can afford. But I do have a scabbard for your sword."

"It belongs to Summer."

Taya turned to her with a smile. "You are so much like my Gale." She brushed bony fingers across Summer's cheek. "You will see that soon enough."

Summer wanted to step back, worried Taya was thinking she'd make a suitable pet. She managed to remain still in case retreating might ruin the negotiations.

"You agree to our terms?" Grayson asked.

"Where is Oliver kept?"

"The doctor has him at the moment," Grayson said.

"I should have known he was with the magic collector." Taya looked from one to the other. "You do realise my magic will bind you to this task."

"I know. We aren't trying to get out of paying our debt to you. We need to return Oliver home where he'll be safe. Both of us will return to you once that's done," Grayson said.

"I agree to the terms."

A sharp, fresh smell filled the chamber. The smell of strawberries and another scent joining it. "Mint?" Summer glanced around the area, unable to figure out the third smell because of the overpowering scent of mint.

Taya nodded once. "Peppermint. Like my mother before me."

"It's the scent of her magic," Grayson said.

"Oh." She'd assumed all magic smelt like strawberries.

"This way." Taya brushed past them and out into the corridor.

Summer lowered her voice. "What does it mean that she's bound us to this task?"

"That we'll be compelled to complete it. We'll have no choice but to take the message to Gale." Grayson gestured towards the doorway. "Let's get going before the light on the phone grows dim."

"I thought the battery would be flat by now." She followed Taya who remained well ahead of them.

"My magic isn't very strong so I'm able to use it to keep some charge in the battery without ruining the phone. But it's losing charge quicker than I can put it in."

"Do you want me to try and do it?"

Grayson shook his head. "Your magic is too strong to be able to do something like that."

"What are we going to tell everyone back home?" She averted her gaze from the missing wall of the corridor, not wanting to know how deep a drop it might be.

"Nothing."

"What do you mean nothing?"

"There's nothing we can tell them that they'll believe. All you have to do is say there is nothing you can tell them."

"They won't believe me."

"They'll have no choice."

She fell silent, having no idea what to say. Her mum would never accept that as an excuse. They needed a better alibi. She was still trying to come up with one that didn't make her feel strange and uncomfortable by the time Taya had led them through the corridors to a ladder attached to a wall, a grate above it.

Taya was wrapping strips of cloth around her hands when they reached her. She pointed to Grayson. "You go up first and open the grate. You've got the least magic to be affected by the iron."

Summer watched as Grayson climbed the ladder and swung the grate open. The light filtering down through the opening was dim. It was either late afternoon or the day had grown cloudy.

Grayson leaned over the edge to peer back down at them. "Come on up."

"You're next." Taya pointed at Summer.

She wasn't about to argue. Being the last one remaining below the ground didn't sound like a good idea. She hissed when her hands wrapped around the rungs. It was worse than when she'd touched the hatch. It felt like a million tiny insects nibbled at her hands, stinging and burning at the same time. She hurried up the ladder, anxious to get away from the pain. It wasn't until she was out in the open that the dizziness hit her at the thought of having climbed out of the chamber. She sat on a nearby rock, trying to control her shaking. She didn't do ladders and had no idea how she'd managed that one. If the trick was to be distracted by pain she wasn't about to make a habit of using that method.

Taya stood over her. "What is wrong with you?"

Grayson stepped between them forcing Taya to move back. "We're hungry. It's been ages since we've eaten."

"Stand up then." Taya held out a closed hand, opening it to reveal a peppermint leaf. Dropping the leaf on the ground, she grabbed hold of their hands. "We'll go to my home first." She stepped on the leaf, the smell of peppermint filling the air.

Chapter Twelve

The world shimmered and reformed and Summer swayed on her feet, standing in front of what looked like a deserted cottage. "Where are we? How did we get here?" Letting go of Taya's hand, she slowly turned around to check out her surroundings. A forest pressed in around the cottage, the small clearing full of tall grass and scattered wildflowers. "Where are the Fringes?"

"There's a well out the back. Draw up some water and clean yourselves before you come inside. There is a tub in the rose garden if you prefer to use that." Taya focused on Summer. "I can bring clothes for you, but he will have to make do with a sheet while his own clothes dry after he washes them." Taya disappeared inside, the door closing behind her.

After staring at the cottage another minute, Summer turned to Grayson. "A rose garden?"

Grayson grinned. "I told you there was more to this realm than the Fringes." He took hold of her hand, the sword in his other. "Let's check it out."

She'd rather go home. "It's so medieval here."

"It's better. They have magic."

Summer stopped when they reached the back of the house. In the middle of the garden was a well, sheltered by a roof with a bucket hanging from the rafter and a timber cap over the top of the stone edge. There was a rose garden off to one side of the well creating a sheltered room, fruit trees towards the back of the clearing and an overgrown vegetable garden on the other side of the well. "This is Taya's place?"

Grayson chuckled. "My thoughts exactly. Who'd expect a bundle of rags to live here?"

"Not me."

Grayson let go of her hand. "I'll get the water and you can check out the tub."

She remained where she was, watching as he walked over to the well and removed the timber cap. How could he be so calm? They had no idea where they were. The Fringes could be anywhere and her brother could be kilometres away.

Grayson unhooked the bucket of water from the rope he'd used to lower it down and fill it. "What's wrong?"

"Where are we?"

"It doesn't matter." He headed for the rose garden.

She hurried after him. "What do you mean it doesn't matter? I have no idea where Oliver is." She entered the garden, having to first go left and then turn right around the roses that created privacy for the tub that looked like it was hewn from a smooth, oval rock, big enough she'd be able to lie full length in it. Again she came to a stop. It was like coming across her dream bathroom. "Did you ever read the story of Hansel and Gretel when you were a little kid?"

He tipped some of the water into the tub to rinse it out before placing a piece of wood, that had been shaped like a cork, into the outlet hole. "Hasn't everyone?"

"Do you get the feeling we've stumbled upon the gingerbread cottage and after we're nice and clean and go inside she's going to shove us in an oven and cook us for dinner?"

Grayson laughed, draping an arm around her shoulders, walking back to the well with her.

She glared at him as he drew up another bucket of water. "I'm serious."

He met her gaze, resting the bucket of water on the edge of the well. "I know. And I didn't mean to laugh. I keep forgetting you don't understand this place. You've actually been pretty calm about it all."

"You can say that after the tunnel?"

"That wasn't to do with the realms of the Fae. That was something else." He glanced towards the cottage. "Come on. We need to get cleaned up for dinner." He grinned again. "Our dinner, not hers."

She watched as he walked away, remaining by the well. He'd have to come back for more water. She waited until he was drawing water again before she spoke. "What is it I don't understand?"

"The binding works both ways. She's as much caught up in what she's agreed to do as we are." He returned to the rose garden with the bucket of water.

Before Summer could go after him and ask more questions, Taya stepped out the back with a basket of folded material and a steaming kettle. She placed them on a timber table by the back door. "To take the chill off the water. If you bring the kettle back to the table I'll boil another lot for the next bath." She returned inside.

While Grayson lugged buckets of water, Summer took the kettle and basket to the rose garden and placed the basket on the mossy cobblestones before tipping the hot water into the tub. She swirled the water around, streaks of dirt left behind.

Grayson joined her with another bucket. "Might want to tip a bucket full of water over yourself first. That water isn't going to stay clean for long if you hop straight in."

"That doesn't sound very pleasant." It actually sounded extremely cold.

"It sounds bracing."

She watched him slip around the roses as she muttered, "Not what I would have said."

When he returned with another bucket of water, he left it on the ground and picked up the kettle. "Don't take too long. Or I might be tempted to join you."

She caught the familiar hint of excitement, mischief and laughter in his eyes and couldn't resist returning his grin as he stepped out of view. Her grin faded as she thought of her brother. Here she was about to soak in the perfect bathtub while her brother was now a cat and locked in a cage, waiting for her to rescue him. It seemed wrong. Glancing skywards, seeing the day was drawing to a close, she hurriedly undressed and, moving away from the tub and basket, tipped the bucket of water over herself.

Grayson was wrong. It wasn't bracing. It was freezing. She brushed some of the dirty water from her body before climbing into the tub. It wasn't much better. The setting might be perfect visually, but the temperature left a lot to be desired. She thought of how hot it had been at the national park, sweat trickling down her back and making her t-shirt stick to her body. Now if only the water had some of that warmth.

The smell of strawberries filled the air and the chill disappeared from the water. She stared at the water, trying to figure out what she'd done. Magic shouldn't be something accidental. What about when she returned home? How many times had she glared at someone who annoyed her, wanting them to slip over or have something undignified happen to them. She couldn't go around making things like that occur.

"Will you be much longer?"

The sound of Grayson's voice startled her. "No." She rubbed at the dirt on her body, wincing as the colour of the water changed. It took a while to untangle her hair from the plait it had been in. The water darkened further. "I don't think I'm going to get very clean."

"Why not?"

His voice was closer than she'd expected and she looked in the direction of the entrance. She couldn't see him. "My hair was full of dirt."

"Put the bucket around the corner and I'll get you another lot of water."

Climbing out of the tub, she shivered at the light breeze, placing the bucket where he'd suggested before stepping away from the rose garden. She pulled the plug and watched as the water swirled away.

When Grayson brought a full bucket, she warmed the water before standing in the tub and tipping it over herself, watching as rivulets of dirt were washed away. It took four more buckets of water before she was clean. She dried herself with one of the towels Taya had placed in the basket. After wrapping the towel around her wet hair, she pulled on a pair of black trousers and a long sleeved, dark red shirt. It had tiny black buttons down the front and the cuffs and hem had patterns embroidered across them in black thread.

"Think you'll be much longer? We're as good as out of daylight."

She looked up at the stars that were starting to appear in the sky, realising by the faint scent of strawberries hanging in the air, that she must have been using her magic to see as the day had stopped growing dark at some point. Gathering up the bucket, she stepped out of the rose garden. Her towel dislodged so that her hair tumbled around her shoulders. "Can't you use your magic to see?"

Grayson stared at her.

"What's wrong?"

He took a step closer, a lantern in one hand. "I forgot how beautiful you are." He grinned. "Didn't you ever wonder why it was you I decided to prank when I was thirteen?" He took the bucket from her.

"Because of the way I looked?" She slid the towel under her hair and around her shoulders, not wanting to get her clothes wet.

He chuckled. "Because I liked you."

"That's lame."

"Yeah, probably." He held out the lantern. "Can you hold this for me so I can see what I'm doing?"

"Why can't you use your magic?"

He strode to the well. "I haven't been able to figure it out. And even if I could figure it out, not all magic can help you see in the dark." After attaching the bucket to the rope, he lowered it into the well. "How do you use it?"

She shrugged, causing the lantern to rock and send light and shadows across the ground and well. "By wanting." She walked beside him to the rose garden and watched as he tipped the bucket into the tub.

"That explanation doesn't help."

"I have no idea how else to explain it." She put her hand in the water and thought of summer days, warming it, the smell of strawberries rising up around her.

"What did you do?"

"Feel it."

Grayson put his hand in the water. "How did you do that?"

"The first time was an accident." She explained it to him as he collected another bucket of water.

This time he tried to warm the water. Unable to, Summer warmed it for him. Nor was he able to warm any of the other buckets of water. He finally gave up, focusing instead on trying to see in the dark. He was no more successful with that.

By the time he'd washed, Summer fetching him an extra two buckets of water, and they'd both washed their clothes, Taya was standing at the back door asking what was taking them so long. Dinner was on the table and going cold.

Summer was surprised to find a vegetable stew served. "Where did you get the food for this?"

Taya gestured towards the back of the cottage. "My garden. It might be overgrown and some of it gone to seed, but there was enough to make a meal. More than enough." She stared past them. "We were getting ready to harvest when he tried to trick me into giving Gale to him. I knew he'd be back. He's not the sort to give up. So we hid from him. We weren't able to hide long enough. I got sick and couldn't keep her hidden. He found us and there was nothing I could do."

Chapter Thirteen

Summer had to stop herself from promising to rescue Gale. Promises were binding around here and the Fae had magic. Far more powerful than what she was able to do. "We'll take your message to her as soon as possible and let you know how she's doing." She wanted to do more.

Taya nodded, returning to eating her food. Once the meal was finished, she stood, eyeing Grayson up and down. "I'll return shortly. Make yourselves comfortable, but touch nothing. I left a scabbard on the bed for you." With a gesture in the direction of the far end of the cottage, she threw down a peppermint leaf and stood on it, disappearing from view, leaving the scent of peppermint in her wake.

"I want to be able to do that." Summer stared at the spot where Taya had been. If she could do that, she'd be able to return to Oliver's side and take him home.

"You'll be able to do it soon."

"Do you think Oliver is okay?"

He reached across the table and held her hand. "Of course he is."

"What if he's scared? Or lonely?"

"You should be more worried about him making friends with the toad in the cage near him. We already have far too many toads at home." He grinned at her, lightly squeezing her hand.

She momentarily returned his grin before frowning. "I wonder what turning into a toad says about someone's personality. And why would anyone bother to rescue someone with that kind of personality?"

"That they're a pest?"

She laughed at his comment, a smile remaining behind. "More than likely. I bet there's a few people I know who'd end up as a toad if they went through a cursed exit." Her smile faded. "How am I going to manage to return home? Iron hurts."

"Gloves. Didn't you see Taya wrap her hands before she climbed up the ladder?"

"Yes, but what about the pain of being near it?"

"Keep your magic levels low. Draw it off and store it in bottles like the doctor stores it."

"You make it sound so simple."

He held her gaze a moment before he spoke. "It won't be simple, but you can make it work if you want to." His hand tightened on hers. "Or you can join me in this realm."

She had no idea what to say. Even opening her mouth didn't help.

"There is no time to be sitting around."

Summer rose from the table, facing Taya, Grayson at her side. "I thought you'd be gone longer."

Taya strode forward and shoved clothes at Grayson. "Dress. We're leaving shortly. We made a deal." She turned to Summer. "Get your sword and scabbard. We're wasting time. So far only I've done anything."

Summer hurried to the bedroom, collecting the scabbard off the bed before leaving Grayson to get dressed in the clothes Taya had given him. The sword was hanging at her side by the time he came out, dressed in black trousers with a white, long sleeved shirt and black vest. "Wow."

"No time to preen. You need to learn how to travel from one place to the next using magic."

Summer faced Taya, more than ready to learn. But it was a lot harder than she expected. Even with someone, who knew what they were doing, to teach her. It took hours for her to create the item, she needed to crush, to take her to the destination of her choice. It was a strawberry flower. She stared at the delicate petals of the flower resting on her palm, the scent of strawberries fading away.

"I did it. I can't believe I finally did it." She held the flower out to Grayson, unable to stop grinning.

"About time," Taya muttered before turning to Grayson. "And what about you? Where is yours? Try again."

Summer listened as Taya again went through the process, trying to teach Grayson. The sky was lightening and light filtered in the windows as the scent of rain filled the room and a stone appeared in his hand, looking like a frozen raindrop. Grayson grinned, continuing to grin even when Taya muttered about useless humans.

"Now what?" Summer asked.

"Now you need to learn the next step." Taya glared at her. "And you better not take days to do so." She led the way outside, pointing to a tree at the edge of the clearing. "That's where I want you to take me. Picture it, pushing all other images from your mind. Then close your eyes and focus on seeing it."

By the time both of them had made several trips to the tree and back to the cottage, using only magic, they were exhausted, the sun high in the sky. Only

Summer had been able to travel without Taya's help and the Fae had warned Grayson against using his magic to travel until it grew in power. She then begrudgingly fed them before transporting them to the doctor's house, having given Summer a cloth bag to carry the bottles of magic.

"I'll wait out here. You're not getting me in there. The magic collector is known to trick magic out of people. I've heard the stories." She crossed her arms over her chest, looking just as bony as ever even though she'd cleaned herself up before bringing them back to the Fringes.

Summer wasn't about to argue. The Fae had nearly driven her crazy with her demands and complaints. Surely she hadn't expected them to learn how to use magic instantly. As Grayson had kept pointing out, it was one of the most difficult things to do. A big step up from heating a bucket of water.

Grayson knocked on the door, putting an arm around Summer's waist. "Not long now."

The door swung open and the doctor stood there, blocking their entrance. "You can't have collected it already."

"Not exactly." Summer held out the bag to him. "There's five and a half bottles."

"You were meant to collect six."

"I don't need the sixth bottle anymore. The half a bottle is because there was some spillage."

The doctor took the crystal out of the bag. "You wasted some of the power of the crystal? And you expect a half a bottle to be enough?"

"It wasn't that much," Grayson said.

"I'll decide how much extra you need, not you." The doctor tried to close the door.

"I want to see my brother." Summer tried to push her way in.

"Not until you've collected more magic." The doctor nearly had the door closed when it swung open, knocking him over, the scent of strawberries filling the air.

"I want to see my brother, now." Summer strode inside, stopping abruptly when she saw only one cage had an occupant. It was the toad. "Where is he?" She glared down at the doctor.

He scrambled to his feet. "This is your fault. I didn't tell you to steal the magic. They took your brother because someone took their brother. Lonan couldn't protect himself because you stole his magic."

She tried to figure out what he meant. "Lonan took my brother?"

The doctor shook his head, backing away. "Perry

took your brother. Lonan's brother, Perry. He said he'd return him when his brother was returned."

"No." Her hair swirled around her in the wind that rose, rapidly growing stronger, the scent of strawberries heavy in the room.

Grayson grabbed hold of her hands and turned her to face him. "We will get him back. But not like this. Someone will know something. They always do around here."

"I'll pay you for the magic," the doctor offered.

Summer pulled away from Grayson, her hand dropping to the hilt of her sword. "You were willing to take it from me and more. You were trying to hide that Oliver is missing."

"I was going to find a way to get him back before you returned with the extra magic."

"He promised to look after him," Grayson said. "He's in our debt for failing to live up to his part of the bargain."

"Let me get some gold for you." The doctor backed away.

"I want my brother. You can keep–"

Grayson interrupted her. "You owe us. A life is worth more than a handful of gold."

"You were the ones who upset powerful Raptors," the doctor said.

"No one should have known he was here. We didn't tell anyone," Grayson said.

"What do you want?" The doctor looked from one to the other.

Summer started to demand the return of her brother, but Grayson interrupted. "We'll start with some gold. And any knowledge you have of Oliver's whereabouts. We'll return later to negotiate the rest of what you owe us. When we know what condition Oliver is in and what needs to be done to rescue him."

"He better be alive and well," Summer threatened.

"You got your own magic out of this bargain. Both of you."

"We wanted one thing from this bargain and it wasn't magic. Now fetch some gold," Grayson ordered.

When the doctor left the room, Summer turned to Grayson, wanting to demand what he thought he was doing.

Grayson shook his head. "Not yet. When we're out of here."

"You better know what you're doing."

He took both of her hands again. "I'd never deliberately do anything to harm your brother."

The doctor came back into the room and held out a handful of coins. Letting go of her hands, Grayson took the coins, not bothering to speak. Taking one of Summer's hands, he marched outside, pocketing the coins. He stopped in front of Taya.

The Fae had her arms crossed over her chest. "I heard. You're not about to get out of what you owe me. You will deliver the message."

"I have to-"

Grayson interrupted Summer again. "Not here. We'll go back to where we were earlier and discuss this."

Summer glared at Grayson. "Will you stop interrupting me all the time?"

Grayson turned to Taya. "Can you take us back so we can sort this out?"

Taya tossed a peppermint leaf onto the ground and grabbed each of them by a hand before stepping on the leaf.

Summer tried to pull away. They didn't have time to discuss anything. She had to go after her brother. The world shimmered around her, reforming to show they were in the clearing at the front of Taya's cottage. "No."

Taya let her go. "You will deliver my letter. I am not at fault for your brother not being there."

Summer closed her hand, focusing on creating a

strawberry flower. Feeling it form, she opened her hand.

Grayson closed her hand, holding it tightly. "We can go after him. It doesn't matter where he is. All you have to do is focus on what he looks like. Hold that image in your mind."

"He could be anywhere. It's dangerous," Taya said. "Only the brave or very stupid travel to a destination using a person rather than a location. You never know where you might end up."

Her brother had the same eyes. "I can do that."

"No." Taya closed her hands over Grayson's preventing him from letting go. "You don't understand how dangerous it is. He could be anywhere. It could be a trap."

She met Taya's brown eyes, ignoring the anger in them. "He's my brother. Would you do any less for Gale?"

Taya let go, taking a step back. "Not even for Gale would I walk into a trap. How would that help her? I'd never throw away all chances of helping her escape. Give up your freedom and then who will go after your brother?"

For a moment she nearly listened to Taya. "What if I leave it too long? He's only a little boy. He must be terrified."

"He's not a boy. He's a cat. The curse has changed him. Don't do this. Or at least take my letter to Gale first."

Her hand tightened on the flower, Grayson's hands still cupping hers. She had no idea what to do. She met Grayson's gaze. There was no mischief in them now. She saw the same fear she felt reflected back at her. "I need to find my brother."

"Picture him. Hold onto me and picture him. I'll go with you."

"You are both crazy. Worse than those with iron sickness." Taya stalked inside, slamming the front door behind her.

"Are we?" She could only whisper the words, afraid Taya was right.

Grayson grinned. "Does it matter if we are?"

She nearly managed a smile in reply. It faded before it had barely begun. "I can't leave him with Perry." Taya didn't know her brother. Didn't know for sure that he wouldn't be scared.

"Picture him. Drop the flower and picture him." He let go of her hand to take her empty one. "Let's get your brother."

Chapter Fourteen

It took Summer a moment before she could reply. "Okay." It was another few seconds before she could uncurl her fingers and let the flower drift to the ground. She stared at it resting amongst the grass. Delicate, snow-white petals surrounding a yellow centre. Taya had told them it could be crushed in the hand, but it was far easier to step on it to travel to places. It took her nearly a minute before she was able to convince herself she could do this. Could track down her brother in whatever location he was in.

Grayson tightened his hand on hers. "Whenever you're ready."

She didn't think she'd ever be ready. But that didn't matter. Lonan's brother had hers and if he was anything like Lonan, she didn't trust him to take care of Oliver. Closing her eyes, she brought to mind the image of her brother's eyes. For a moment she saw the hazel eyes in the face of a boy, messy blond hair and a mischievous grin. The image transformed into a white cat, the eyes remaining the same. Opening her eyes, she stepped on the flower, the world shimmering around her to reform again.

For a split second she stared into her brother's eyes before the ground dropped out beneath her and Grayson's hand was pulled from her grip. She fell past a rock wall, reaching for it as panic raced through her body. Her fingers scraped over the wall, then a cliff face of rusty red sandstone before she crashed onto a ledge. The impact wasn't as hard as she'd expected. Grayson fell on top of her. It happened so fast she didn't have the chance to scream. A cloud of dust settled around them, the scent of strawberries mixing with the smell of dirt.

She faced a sandstone cliff, nothing else visible, her body surprisingly unharmed after the fall. She tried to hang onto the image of her brother's eyes, but the sensation of falling clung to her and her stomach somersaulted making her want to throw up. She needed to know where she was and where her brother was. Taking a deep breath, coughing from the dust, Summer started to turn.

Grayson stopped her, his hand covering her eyes, an arm preventing her from moving. "Stay still."

"What are you doing? Let go of me." She fought the panic that threatened to overwhelm her.

He shifted so his body pinned hers down. "Summer. Trust me. Stay very still."

The tone of his voice made her freeze. "I need to see."

"No you don't."

"Grayson–" Her voice broke on his name. She tried again, afraid to find out what he was keeping from her. "Grayson, let me see."

He moved his hands, his face above hers, his hands cupping her face so she could only see him. "You need to remain calm. Understand?"

"I'm not going to remain calm if I can't see where I am." The images that flashed through her mind weren't in the least bit comforting and she began to shake harder.

"I'll tell you where we are, but I need you to promise me you won't scream. A binding promise. That for however long it takes us to get Oliver away from here you won't scream."

"Can we do that? Use our magic to make a promise?"

"Try."

"Okay. I promise not to scream until we get Oliver away from here."

"Will it. Wish for it. Whatever you do to use your magic."

She concentrated on wanting her words to be true, smiling when the smell of strawberries mixed with the scent of rain. "We did it." For a few seconds the triumphant feeling made her forget the sensation of falling. It rushed back in on her and she shuddered, momentarily closing her eyes as she tried to get past it.

"He's in a castle. I'm guessing a dungeon since it's the lowest level and there are bars on the window. He was looking out the window, his face pressed against the bars."

"How could there be bars? I didn't feel the pain of iron."

"The Fae have their own metals they can use. Like what they use for their swords. No iron needed."

"Okay, so he's in a dungeon. We just have to look inside the dungeon and transport ourselves in there like we did in Taya's clearing." Her shaking started to subside. They could do this. Rescue her brother and take him back to Taya who'd turn him into a boy again.

"Not exactly. The castle is overlooking a-" Grayson broke off, frowning. "I didn't consider that."

"What?"

"We can't lie. Like the Fae, magic will prevent us from lying."

"You were going to lie to me?" She tried to push him away from her.

His body continued to hold hers down. "Not lie exactly. I wanted to say valley, but I suppose valleys are green. This is red sand."

"Like a canyon?" Her stomach did a long slow turn and she felt light headed.

"That wasn't the word I'd planned to use."

"But is it the word that suits?" She wanted to beg him to say no. Either that or let her look for herself so she could see it wasn't true. "Grayson? What word suits?"

"They've built their castle in the perfect location so they can see if enemies are approaching."

Her stomach lurched and she tried to turn away from him. "I'm going to be sick." She managed to turn her head, catching a glimpse of a dizzying drop before his hands were back in place. She opened her mouth to scream, but nothing came out. Not the slightest sound.

"You're not going to be sick. Look at me. Don't think about where we are. Focus on me."

It didn't help. Her light-headedness grew worse

and her stomach spun out of control. "You're not that good a distraction."

"Really?"

"No." She glared at him.

A smile fleetingly appeared before Grayson lowered his head and his lips met hers.

Surprise kept her momentarily still. Her hands that had been pushing him away crept around his neck. The light-headedness remained, but her stomach quit its acrobatics. When he pulled back slightly, continuing to block her vision, she smiled wryly. "That wasn't exactly what I was expecting."

"Did it help?"

Laughter was surprised from her. "Not as much as I wish." She stared up at him, reassured by the almost familiar look in his eyes. Surely the situation couldn't be that bad with the hint of excitement, mischief and laughter she could see in them. Maybe he'd misjudged how far above them the barred window was. "I like it when your eyes look like that."

"Like what?"

She was disappointed that the look was replaced by curiosity. "Like there's a joke you know and you're keeping it all to yourself. Or something good is about to happen. I saw it in your eyes when you played that prank on me."

"I wouldn't exactly have called that good."

She relaxed a little. "It wasn't that bad. After the initial shock I was kind of glad for the coolness of the water." When he continued to stare at her, remaining silent, his expression unreadable, she spoke. "What are you thinking?"

"That I wish I'd had the courage to talk to you instead of dumping water over you back when I was thirteen."

"You were scared to talk to me?"

Grayson grinned. "Terrified. I couldn't stop looking at you and every time you looked in my direction I pretended to be looking somewhere else in case you spoke to me. I had no idea what I'd say and feared my voice would break and all that would come out was a squeak."

"Really?" She started to shake her head, but was prevented by his hands that cupped her face. "You seemed so confident. The other boys followed your lead and listened to everything you said."

"We can't lie, remember?"

"That's going to be a problem when we return home."

Grayson chuckled. "We'll have to learn to be as crafty as the Fae. Distraction or cleverly worded comments. We'll get the hang of it."

Fear rushed in on her at the reminder of the Fae. "What's wrong?"

"We're on a cliff."

"How much do you want to save your brother?"

"Can't you go and get him out of the dungeon? You saw it, didn't you?" She'd been too focused on her brother's eyes.

"I don't get it right every time. Do you really want me to be the one to take your brother out of there?"

She closed her eyes, opening them when his lips brushed across hers. "What are we going to do?"

"You have magic."

"I know. But how is that going to help me get off a cliff when the thought of it makes me want to scream." She tried not to tremble, but the word cliff had her breathing faster and panic racing through her body. "Grayson–"

"Are you bruised?"

"I want to go home." Tears welled and she tried to keep them from falling. "I want my brother and I want to go home."

"Do I need to kiss you again?"

"You're not that good a distraction."

"So you tried to tell me."

She almost returned his smile. Taking a deep breath, she tried to focus on his blue eyes. It didn't help. The solid ground beneath her, several pebbles digging into her back, reminded her that she wasn't in a safe location.

"Summer, you used magic before you hit the ground."

"No I-" she couldn't speak the rest of the sentence, the words refusing to come. "Why can't I say that I didn't?"

"Because it'd be a lie. Your body knows you used magic. Automatically used the air to cushion your landing. Stirred up a tonne of dust too."

"I thought that was from landing."

"Not that amount of dust. Trust me. I've fallen out of enough trees over the years to know."

"Why would you climb a tree? That's crazy."

"Because it's fun."

Her stomach twisted at the thought of falling out of a tree. Her arms went around him. "You could have hurt yourself. Broken your neck or something."

"Why are you terrified of heights?"

She frowned, trying to figure out the answer. "I can't think of a time when I wasn't."

"So there's no logical reason."

"Of course there's a logical reason. Falling hurts."

"Does it?"

"Okay, maybe I can use magic to cushion my fall, but that won't work if I pass out."

"So don't pass out."

"Easy for you to say. I go light headed and dizzy and the next thing I know I'm waking up somewhere else. Usually in a bed with someone staring worriedly at me." She'd lost count of the amount of times that had happened. Each time she'd nearly died of embarrassment. In the end it had been easier to avoid all heights. To say she'd forgotten to eat and must have got dizzy from hunger. That always got rid of the worried expression and caused a lecture instead. Far easier to cope with that than all the fussing.

"Don't you want to save your brother?"

Chapter Fifteen

Before Summer had a chance to answer, she heard the sound of a cat miaowing. Was that Oliver? It was followed by the sharp voice of a man.

"Don't go wrapping yourself around my legs like that. There's no food for you. The only reason I keep coming in here is to check on you. Except this time. Perry is sick of waiting. It's time for you to die." There was the sound of footsteps moving quickly and a cat hissing. "Get back here. Running won't help."

No one was killing her brother. "Get off me." She pushed at Grayson, a rush of air following her movements and he fell back, scrambling away from the edge. Standing up, she barely glanced towards the sheer drop as she listened to the man threaten her brother, chasing him around the dungeon. She opened her hand, a flower already in it.

"I'm going with you." Grayson grabbed hold of her arm.

The flower drifted to the red, sandy ledge they stood on and she stepped on it the moment it landed, picturing her brother's eyes. The world shimmered and reformed as a dimly lit cell with a cat skidding to a halt at their feet, a Raptor throwing himself to the side and crashing into a wall in an effort not to run into them.

Summer started to draw her sword.

Grayson scooped up Oliver. "No. The clearing. Take us back to the clearing." He grabbed hold of her arm.

She formed another flower, managing to step on it as the Raptor threw himself towards them, sword drawn. Her heart raced and her breath came in gasps as the clearing came into focus. She clung to Grayson, Oliver pressed between them. No one else was in the clearing. "We're safe?"

Grayson glanced over his shoulder as the cottage door opened. "Maybe not. I don't think Taya looks happy."

Summer let go of Grayson, taking Oliver with her. He was right. Taya didn't look happy. "I have my brother."

"What took you so long? Another day has nearly

finished. Are you trying to waste time? How long are you going to make me wait?"

Grayson scooped Oliver out of Summer's arms. "Break the curse and we'll take him home. Then it will be time for us to visit Gale."

"Bring him inside. Put him on the bed." Taya stalked back inside, leaving the door open.

When Grayson started to follow, Summer grabbed his arm. "Are you sure this is safe?"

"How else are we going to break the curse?"

Her eyes narrowed. "You don't know, do you?"

"What makes you say that?"

"Because you haven't answered my question. You're avoiding it without lying."

Grayson grinned. "At least we know that works."

She glared at him. "Tell me. Is this safe?"

"There's always a risk with magic, but the only other option is to leave him as a cat. Do you really want that?"

"No." She let go of his arm. "I want him safe at home in his normal form. I also don't want him to remember anything about the Fae. I don't want him coming back here ever again."

"He'll forget one day. On his twenty-first birthday."

"That's not good enough. I want him to forget

now. He's too curious. I don't want him coming back here getting into more trouble."

Grayson stared at her silently for a moment. "Let's deal with this problem for now. We can figure out the other one later if you want."

"Were you trying to figure out a way to say that without lying to me?"

Grayson chuckled. "Are you going to be examining every word I say in future? You do know I could have told you a million lies before we had magic and you never would have known."

"Did you?"

"Not a million." He grinned, striding towards the cottage.

She hurried after him. "How many were there?"

"Most of them were in the tunnel." He frowned. "Maybe all of them. I'm not sure now."

She sighed. "This is going to make life so difficult. What do I say when my friends ask me how something looks on them and it doesn't suit them at all?"

"That you prefer a different garment?"

"That might work. How did you think of that so quickly?"

"I've practised lying without actually lying lots of times. I've always known I wanted this." He entered the bedroom and placed Oliver on the bed, resting a hand on the cat when he wanted to jump off.

Taya pushed Grayson out of the way and pointed a bony finger at Oliver. "You stay there. Lie down."

Oliver obeyed, his tail flicking a couple of times.

The room was filled with the scent of Taya's magic and Oliver stretched out, his body continuing to stretch and reform, turning into that of a blond haired boy, his eyes closed as he rolled onto his side, tucking his hand under his cheek.

"He's okay?" Summer took half a step towards her brother.

"He'll sleep for about five hours. You might want to get him home before he wakes. Pesky human boy. They always find trouble." Taya stalked out of the room and rummaged around in her kitchen.

Summer was tempted to ask for a meal, but doubted Taya would feed them. Not after her complaints the last time. "Where do we take him?"

"Think you can return us to the doctor's? Or the courtyard marketplace. I can show you the way from either of those places."

"Yes. Either one. I could also take us back to the grate where we entered the tunnel."

"The courtyard marketplace then." Grayson slung

Oliver over his shoulder. The boy murmured in his sleep.

Summer brushed Oliver's hair back from his face, holding it out of the way to stare at his peaceful expression. "He looks the same as always." After all that had happened she could barely believe the curse was broken.

Grayson took her hand. "He will be himself." He grinned. "Which according to the doctor was pretty much like a cat. Curious, playful, affectionate, adventurous and caring."

She let Oliver's hair fall back into place, closing her hand to form a strawberry flower. "As long as he doesn't start catching mice it'll be all good." She let the flower fall to the floor. "Are you ready?"

He tightened his grip on her hand. "Yes."

She met his gaze for a moment before she nodded, pictured the part of the courtyard marketplace where'd they'd sat by the fire, then stepped on the flower. Night had fallen when they arrived and firelight flickered nearby.

"You've got to be kidding."

Summer looked in the direction Grayson stared, fear exploding through her. "Raptors."

"Come on." Turning away, he tugged on her hand, leading her into a nearby alley.

"Is this the way we need to go?"

"It'll get us there."

"So it's not?"

"Quiet. Listen to what's around us."

She did, surprised at how many sounds she was able to notice. There were Fae nearby. She heard the soft murmur of voices, footsteps and someone coughing. Even closer was laboured breathing, broken by a groan. She thought of the first time she'd been at the courtyard marketplace and the Fae who'd been stabbed. It seemed impossible that it was only a day ago. How much time would have passed back in her world?

The alleys they hurried through became narrower and the cobblestones more uneven and broken. Summer stumbled, pressing a hand against a wall to prevent herself from falling. "Where are we going?"

"To the exit we should have used the first time."

"I'm sorry I didn't listen."

Grayson glanced over his shoulder. "I'm not." He fleetingly grinned.

She stared at his back, wondering why. Was it because he now had magic? Before she could ask, he stopped at a hole in the wall, placing Oliver on the ground, leaning him against the wall near the hole. "What are you doing?"

"We have to go through here. Do you need help?"

"Is it a drop?"

"No. But I need you to go first so I can hand Oliver through to you."

"Okay." She climbed in the hole, glad of her ability to see in the dark. Everything was shadowy, but she had a feeling it would normally be pitch black. She climbed out of the narrow tunnel into a cave that wasn't much wider, a warm breeze rushing over her. She was pretty sure the breeze was why Grayson's clothes had been dry last time he came back from the realms of the Fae. "Hand him through." She reached for her brother's feet, tugging him towards her. Once Oliver was out of the tunnel, Grayson climbed through and picked Oliver up, after nearly tripping over him in the dark. "Is it much further?"

"We're at the national park. Look up."

She did and saw a narrow strip of stars above her. "We're in the cliff?"

Grayson didn't get a chance to reply. "Grayson? Is that you?" A torch was turned on and pointed in their direction.

Summer shielded her eyes from the light. "Turn it off. Or at least face it at the ground."

"Spencer?" Grayson pushed past her, carrying

Oliver. "What are you doing here? How long has it been?"

"Five days."

Summer's stomach lurched at Spencer's words. "Mum and Tim must be frantic."

"They're not the only ones," Spencer said dryly.

"What are you doing here?" Grayson asked again.

"We've been taking turns waiting for you." Spencer led the way through the passages. "It's nearly morning. They'll be out here searching for the three of you soon."

"How did you get out here?" Grayson asked.

"Frank gave me a lift."

Chapter Sixteen

Summer felt light headed, but in a different way to when she was staring down a long distance. More dizzy and confused. "Who is Frank?"

"One of our older cousins. He's twenty. He went through behind you, but couldn't see any of you. Where were you?" Spencer looked back at them, momentarily shining the torch in their direction. "He's waiting at the car park."

Grayson pushed the torch aside. "Stop doing that. Are you trying to blind me?" He paused a moment. "Oliver went through a cursed exit and we had to get the curse broken."

"You're not coming back, are you?" Spencer asked. "You've figured out how you can stay."

Summer wanted to tell Grayson he had to. She couldn't return home on her own.

"I'm not staying in the realms of the Fae just yet. Eventually, but not yet."

Summer stepped through the last of the passageways, taking in deep breaths of warm air. It was going to be a hot day. "We have to go back. We made a promise to help someone."

"Are you crazy?" Spencer shone the torch at his brother again.

"Will you quit doing that?" Grayson set Oliver on the ground, laying him down once he brushed away some small rocks. "He'll be awake in less than five hours. We have to return."

Spencer grabbed Grayson's arm before he could step back into the passageway. "Why did you make a promise? What happened?"

"We had to get help to break the curse. Now we have to hold up our end of the bargain."

"Is it dangerous?" Spencer kept a hold of Grayson's arm.

Grayson grinned. "When has the realms of the Fae ever been safe?"

Spencer started to smile. It faded before it had barely formed. "You have magic, don't you?"

"What makes you ask that?"

"Because you haven't practised talking like the Fae in ages. And never to me."

"Yeah. I have magic."

"Are you sure you're coming back?"

Summer wanted to say that of course he was coming back. But the words wouldn't come. It was impossible for her to lie.

Grayson shook his brother's hand off his arm, placing his own on Spencer's shoulder. "You know I never planned to remain in this world."

"I know. But I thought there'd be more time. That you'd wait until a day or two before your twenty-first birthday."

"I was waiting until I had the skills and the gear to survive in the realms of the Fae."

Spencer didn't speak straight away. "You have that now, don't you?"

When Grayson nodded, Summer wanted to beg him to stay in the human world. He turned towards her as if he felt her gaze on him.

He smiled. "I'll visit here, but it isn't home."

She wanted more than visits. Raising her hand, she nearly pressed her fingers against her lips, remembering their kisses. Instead she lowered it again. "We have to go back. We told Taya we'd help her once Oliver was safely home."

"Technically he's not home yet." Grayson grinned at her before he faced his brother. "Take Oliver back to his parents. Remind him not to tell them about the Fae. Although I doubt they'd believe him." He held out Summer's phone. "Put this in his pocket. The battery is flat so it's of no use to us."

She wanted to protest. What would her parents think when they found it on Oliver?

"What do I tell them?" Spencer took the phone.

"That you couldn't sleep and talked Frank into driving you out here for a walk. Brush away our footprints once we're gone and say that you found him here. Asleep." Grayson slowly shook his head. "There's nothing else you can tell them that they'd believe."

"Will I see you again?" Spencer stared at his brother.

Grayson grinned. "Of course you will." He opened up his hand, holding it out to his brother. A stone raindrop rested there. "Call me and I'll see if I can figure out how to come to you. I'm not very good at magic yet." He glanced towards Summer before returning his gaze to his brother. "But just in case I figure out how to make it work, be somewhere where I can appear out of nowhere without scaring anyone."

Spencer took the stone, closing his hand over it. "This feels like goodbye."

"I'm sorry."

Grayson's words made her think of when he'd said them to her. She moved to his side, taking his hand. "Can we return from here?" She opened her other hand to reveal a flower.

"You have magic too?" Spencer asked.

She shrugged slightly. "It wasn't planned."

"You're both staying back there?"

She tried to tell him no, frowning when the word wouldn't come. Panic raced through her. She didn't want to live in the realms of the Fae. Images came to her mind. The rose garden, the clearing, the courtyard marketplace. So many fascinating places. "My family would be devastated if I never returned home."

"You're staying," Spencer said.

"I never said that." She glared at him, annoyed he'd pointed it out.

Grayson grinned down at her. "You're staying with me?"

"Of course I have to go back and help Taya."

"If you're not staying, you could have easily said no." Grayson continued to grin.

It was impossible to say the word 'no'. Looking away from Grayson's knowing look, she spoke to

Spencer. "I don't know how long we'll be gone." She let the flower drift to the ground.

"Be careful."

She nodded in reply to Spencer's words and stepped on the flower, taking her and Grayson to the clearing.

The moment they arrived, Grayson let go of her hand to tug her against him, wrapping his arms around her. "You're staying with me?"

She stared up at him, still unable to say 'no'. "I have no idea. I should return home."

"That sounds like you don't really want to."

"There are interesting places here."

"And interesting people?"

She laughed at his comment, the laughter cut off by his kiss.

"You are wasting time."

Smiling, Summer turned in Grayson's arms to face Taya. Nothing the Fae said could wreck her good mood. Her brother was safe. "We need a destination if you want us to deliver a message to Gale."

"I can take you close, and show you where you have to go, but it will be up to you to go the rest of the way. I have a painting of Gale. You will need to know who to deliver the letter to." Taya stepped backwards, out of the doorway.

They followed her inside, Grayson's arm remaining around Summer's waist. Taya told them to wait in the kitchen while she fetched the painting from her room. It was about the size of a normal photograph, painted on a canvas and framed by dark timber.

Summer took the painting and stared at the girl who looked to be around her age. She was smiling, her eyes bright with laughter, a sword in a scabbard and wearing a red jacket, unbuttoned to show a white shirt that tucked into her black trousers. This was Gale? It wasn't what she'd expected. The girl was stunning and looked like she knew how to handle the weapon she wore. She handed the painting to Grayson.

"No wonder another Fae wanted her." He looked up from the painting, meeting Taya's gaze. "You Fae tend to collect beauty."

Summer felt momentarily irritated that he thought Gale was beautiful. She took the painting from him and handed it back to Taya. "Where's the letter you want us to deliver?"

Taya placed the painting on the kitchen table and drew a folded piece of cream paper from her pocket. There was a drop of wax holding it shut, a seal having been pressed into it. "Only give it to her when she is alone and wait for a reply. Bring the reply straight back to me."

Nodding, Summer took the letter and tucked it in a pocket. "I don't suppose we can have something to eat before you take us there."

"It is halfway through the next day and you want to waste yet more time?"

"We weren't gone that long," Summer said.

"Then you shouldn't need to eat," Taya said.

"We were hungry before we left."

Grayson put a hand on Summer's arm, ending the rest of the words she'd been about to speak. "It might help us concentrate better. We're new to magic."

Grumbling, Taya made them sandwiches with salad and thick slices of freshly baked bread, glaring at them while they ate. When they eventually said they were ready to go, she muttered, "About time." Dropping a peppermint leaf on the floor, she grabbed them by the hand and took them to the edge of a forest. Letting go of their hands, she pointed towards a castle sitting on a hill, the trees ending about halfway up, leaving open meadows leading up to the castle. "She's in there."

"In a castle?" That was the last place Summer had expected. "How are we meant to find her in there?"

Taya grinned. A rather unfriendly one. "That will

be your problem. You have no choice other than to complete your part of the bargain." She threw a leaf on the ground, stepped on it, and disappeared leaving behind the scent of peppermint that was rapidly fading.

Summer stared off into the distance. "How are we meant to get into a castle?"

"We're going to have to figure it out." Grayson took hold of her hand, pointing at a tree a fair distance from them with his other hand. "Think you can travel there?"

"Even if I use magic to travel from location to location it's still going to take us ages to get to the castle."

Grayson grinned, the familiar look in his eyes. "Good thing we had something to eat first."

She glared at him before throwing a strawberry flower on the ground and taking them to the tree he'd pointed to. She misjudged and they ended up pressed against the tree when they arrived, stumbling backwards in an effort not to fall over. "That wasn't a good start."

"At least we didn't end up inside the tree."

She stared at him, mouth open.

Grayson pressed under her jaw, closing her mouth and grinning at her.

She took a step back, letting go of his hand she'd continued to clutch. "You're kidding, right?"

"No."

"Why didn't you say something before?" Panic rushed through her and she took more steps away from him. "I can't do this. What if I get us killed?"

"You haven't yet."

"But what if–"

"You won't." He stepped close, taking both her hands, his grip tightening when she tried to pull away. "I trust you."

She stared up at him, surprised by his words. "You can't lie."

"I know."

"How could you trust me? I barely know what I'm doing."

"You're a lot better at this than you think. A natural."

"Probably that overdose of magic I had," she muttered.

"That would have helped." He paused a moment. "Are you going to stay with me?"

"You're not going to keep asking that question are you?"

"I plan to keep asking until you answer with a yes or no."

She had no idea why she was so torn between the two options. It should be a simple no. "I need to return to my family after we deliver Gale's reply to Taya."

"But are you coming back?"

Chapter Seventeen

It took Summer a moment to answer. "I really don't know. I keep thinking I should stay in the human world. That is the place I belong. But I don't know where I belong anymore."

"Do you wish you'd never come here?"

She thought of everything that had happened. Including her brother being turned into a cat, facing Lonan, being stuck in a tunnel and using magic to travel to different destinations. Taya had told them that some people were capable of travelling to places they'd never visited before or hadn't seen, with only the help of a picture. That sounded pretty cool to her. "No. I'm glad I came. Glad I came here with you."

He crushed her to him, kissing her before drawing back. "I want you to stay here with me."

"I know, but I can't answer that question. I don't

think I can until after I return to my family. I need to figure out where my place is."

"Mind if I help you figure it out?"

She tried to work out what he meant, but couldn't. "How would you do that?"

He grinned at her. "I guess you'll have to wait and see."

She recognised the look in his eyes. "You're planning something."

"What makes you say that?"

"I can see it in your eyes."

Grayson laughed. "My mum accuses me of that too."

She couldn't resist smiling. At least it gave her a warning. "Buckets of cold water better not be involved."

"How about buckets of warm water?" He lowered his voice. "And a tub of stone surrounded by roses. And us."

She could only meet his gaze, lost for words. It sounded far too tempting.

He fleetingly kissed her before drawing back. "Let's get this over and done with so we can get on with more interesting things."

Now that was something she could agree on. "Yes." She took his hand. "Where to next?"

They slowly crossed the countryside, having to walk once the daylight faded from the sky. Summer had feared the reduced light would make it harder to pick the correct location. She didn't want to end up inside a tree or rock. That would have to be worse than standing at the top of a cliff.

When they reached the edge of the forest, the meadow stretching out in front of them, Grayson tried to talk her into using her magic to take them to the castle wall. She continued to refuse until he pointed out the archers on the battlements. None of them had drawn bows, but they scanned the night for movement, in between pacing back and forth.

Taking a deep breath, Summer tried to convince herself that she could take them to the castle wall without getting stuck in it. But she didn't know. She was exhausted and making a flower form in her closed hand took a lot longer than it had the last time. Was there a limit to how much magic could be used? She was tempted to ask Grayson, but feared the answer might prevent her from ever wanting to use it again.

Wrapping her arms around Grayson, she stepped on the flower that she'd dropped on the ground between them, closing her eyes to help bring the image of the castle wall to mind. She had studied a section where a tower jutted out, creating a slightly different angle, so that hopefully she'd reach the location she wanted, rather than one that vaguely looked like it. Taking them to the wrong destination once in a day was more than enough. Luckily when she'd made that mistake earlier it had brought them closer to the castle, not further away.

After stepping on the flower, she swayed on her feet, wanting to drop with exhaustion. She opened her eyes to see if she'd brought them to the right location. Relief rushed through her.

"Are you okay?"

She tried to say yes. Her magic wouldn't let her. "Will I have to speak the truth for the rest of my life?"

Grayson chuckled softly. "Yep."

"It's so annoying."

"What's wrong? I guess you were about to lie to me about how you feel."

"Tired." Completely and utterly exhausted and feeling like she might pass out. At least the magic didn't make her elaborate.

"We'll have a rest once we've found Gale." Taking her hand, and keeping close to the wall, Grayson walked towards the gate. They stopped well before reaching it, seeing two guards behind the barred gate.

"How are we meant to get in there?"

"I could try and take us there, but I can't promise it'll go well," Grayson said.

She bit back the complaints she wanted to make, sagging against his side. "How did Taya expect us to find a single person in such a large place?"

"I don't think she cared about that part. It's our problem since we agreed to the bargain."

"Remind me in future to ask more questions before I go making any deals."

"Does that mean you're planning to stay?"

She met his gaze, returning his smile. "It means that I'll at least visit."

He was silent a moment. "The Fae live longer than humans."

"I guessed that after some of the things I've heard while being here."

"It's their magic."

It took her a few seconds to make the connection. Her mouth dropped open, Grayson tapping her under the chin so that she closed it. She slowly shook her head, trying to grasp what it would mean. "How much longer?"

"It varies."

"What's the oldest Fae you've heard of?"

"I don't know their age, only that they're centuries

old." Grayson grinned, tapping her under the chin again.

"What am I going to tell my parents? My brother? I'll outlive everyone."

"Not everyone."

Her mind was a whirl of questions, confusion and half formed sentences. "Why don't more of your family get magic? Don't they want to live forever?"

"It's not the living forever part they object to. It's living in the realms of the Fae or the problems of having magic in the human realm."

She slowly shook her head again. "I can't deal with this right now. I'll figure it out once I'm home again."

"Okay." He glanced towards the gate. "What are we going to do about getting in there?"

She stared at a shadowy corner she could see well past the gate. "Don't let me fall." She dropped a flower on the ground between them and wrapped her arms around him, not relocating them until he held her equally as tight. When she became aware of her surroundings again, she was sprawled across Grayson's chest and he was sitting in the shadows with his back against a stone wall. "I passed out?"

"Seems that way."

"That can't be good."

"I wouldn't think so."

"Is it safe here?"

Grayson chuckled softly. "One day you might stop asking that about this realm."

She lightly hit his chest. "You know what I mean."

"No, Summer, it's as far from safe as you can get. One of the guards walked past here before. It was only that he heard a noise behind him that he didn't find us. We need to move away from here."

She tried to get to her feet. In the end Grayson had to help her. "Why am I so exhausted? My body feels drained."

"Maybe we should have walked instead of using your magic to reach the edge of the forest. We've still got to return to Taya's cottage after we've found Gale." Grayson took part of her weight, his arm around her waist as he helped her walk further into the castle grounds.

"Don't remind me."

They tried to find an entrance into the castle. Avoiding guards and staying to the shadows kept them far from any entrance and they ended up in the extensive gardens that were behind the castle. Lanterns were hung throughout the gardens, making it more difficult to hide. They slipped behind a hedge that ran along a wall of a picturesque building, remaining huddled in the shadows, waiting for a guard to continue along his route. He didn't move. A Fae woman joined him, holding his hand and smiling up at him as she spoke softly.

Summer didn't realise she'd drifted off to sleep until the sounds of laughter woke her, early morning light barely reaching them through the shelter of the hedge. She tried to stretch, disturbing Grayson. "Do you think we can quit hiding in here? Parts of me feel numb from sitting all night."

"Someone might see us."

She groaned, wriggling as she tried to get comfortable. "How are we going to find Gale when we're stuck here?"

"I don't think you're going to like the answer to that."

"You better not say we have to wait until night." She glared at him when he remained silent. There was no way she could remain behind the hedge all day. She was uncomfortable, hungry, thirsty and needed to use a bathroom.

Grayson cupped his hands together, moisture slowly filling them, the faint scent of rain on the air around them.

"What are you doing?"

"I'm thirsty."

"How are you doing that?"

"By taking the moisture from the air. My magic is more drawn to water, not air like yours."

"Why are they different?"

"Because yours comes from a Raptor and most of mine comes from you." He drank the water that had pooled in his hands.

"That doesn't make sense."

"Of course it does. You must be drawn to the water. Or at least have an affinity for it." He gestured towards her hands. "Do you want a drink?"

She cupped her hands, watching as they slowly filled with water. "We live not far from the beach and I spend a lot of time there." She drank the water, surprised at how fresh it tasted. She leaned against Grayson. "We can't stay here all day. I need to find a bathroom at some stage. Very soon."

Chapter Eighteen

Summer and Grayson remained silent, watching as the gardens began to fill with people. After a while they decided to chance wandering through the crowds, hoping they weren't noticed amongst those in the gardens. It didn't take them long to find a bathroom, but after several hours of searching they hadn't found Gale.

Summer finished eating the last of the fruit they'd pilfered from a table laden with food. "She could be anywhere."

Grayson grabbed hold of her arm and pulled her into a nearby arbour. "It's worse than that."

"What do you mean?" She turned to look in the direction Grayson stared in. "How are we meant to give her a letter when she's surrounded by all those people?"

"I've got a feeling those people are the ones who own the castle by the way they're being treated."

She feared he was right. "We're going to be caught."

"No we aren't. We'll follow from a distance."

Summer watched as the group got a little ahead of Gale, who'd stopped to pick a rosebud. "We'll never get across the gardens without being noticed. Not now there are less people about."

"A pity you can't send the letter to her on the wind. Someone would notice it flying through the gardens."

She turned to stare at Grayson, an idea forming. "No, not the letter."

Grayson grinned. "Your voice."

"Yes." The look in his eyes had her thinking they had a good chance of success. She tugged a gentle breeze to her, whispering Gale's name into it before sending it across the gardens, releasing it near the girl who'd begun to walk again.

Gale froze, looking around the gardens with a puzzled expression on her face.

Summer pulled another breeze to her, sending Gale's name on it. This time she released it to the side of the girl and watched as she walked towards it, peering behind a hedge.

"It's working. Do it again," Grayson said.

Summer continued to gather the breezes, sending Gale's name on them, drawing the girl closer. She'd nearly reached them when she stopped abruptly, looking around. Fearing Gale was about to turn away, she sent Taya's name on the next breeze, watching the startled expression that appeared on Gale's face before she hurried towards their hiding place.

Grayson half stepped out of the arbour when Gale was close. "Over here."

Gale slipped into the shadows with them. "Who are you?"

Summer held out the sealed letter. "Taya sent us."

Gale pressed the letter to her chest. "She's well? I thought she was lost to iron sickness."

"She's improving." Grayson nodded towards the letter. "We have to take a reply back to her."

Gale slipped the letter into the bodice of her dress. "I need to return to the group. Will you wait here for me? I'll slip back after dark."

"Here or behind the hedge over near that building." Grayson pointed to where they'd hid earlier.

"Thank you for bringing me the letter." Gale hurried away without a single backwards glance.

Summer stared after her. "We better not get caught."

"Maybe you should have a flower ready in case we have to leave in a hurry."

"You have one of your little rocks ready in case we're separated. We'll meet back at the clearing if we are." She slipped the flower into her pocket, hoping it didn't break.

Grayson put a stone in his pocket then formed another one and held it out to her. "This is the Fae's equivalent to a mobile phone. Although it's only one way. Speak against it and I'll hear the words like a whisper on the breeze. Don't say my name or the rock will travel to me. If you do need me urgently, whisper my name against it and break it."

"What if you want to reply?"

"Then you'll have to give me one of your flowers."

She took the stone, formed one of her flowers and gave it to him. Holding the stone against her lips, she turned her back on him and whispered against the stone, asking if he could hear her. She smiled when she heard him whisper 'yes' back to her. She faced him. "Can anyone else hear what you say?"

"No. Only you."

"That's pretty cool."

"Does it make you want to stay?"

She grinned, moving closer. "It'll take more than a few tricks to convince me to stay."

"Do you want to be convinced?" He reached for her, tugging her into his arms.

She thought about it for a moment. "I don't know."

Grayson drew her down beside him when he sat on the bench seat. "We don't have to stay here permanently."

She met his gaze, trying to read his expression in the shadowy arbour. When the area brightened, a hint of strawberries filling the air, she smiled.

"What's funny?"

"People are going to wonder why they keep smelling strawberries when I'm around. I tend to use my magic automatically."

Grayson chuckled. "I do too, but for the minor things you can barely smell the rain. At least people won't keep looking at the sky when you're around. You can pass it off as perfume."

They fell silent, leaning against each other as they waited for Gale. Several times Summer drifted off to sleep, jarred awake by the sounds of people in the area. As the day progressed, Grayson fetched more food while Summer waited in the arbour and they took turns at using the bathroom. They were worried that if they both left they'd miss Gale's return.

Gale joined them after sunset, lanterns once again lit throughout the gardens. She stopped in front of them, holding out a sealed letter to Grayson. "I want to thank you for bringing me news of Taya." She rested her hand on Grayson's wrist when he took the letter.

Summer wanted to push her away while at the same time tell her that she was the one who'd brought them to the castle.

Grayson drew his arm away from her, putting the letter in his pocket before he slid his arm around Summer's waist. "We were only fulfilling our part of a bargain."

"I still want to thank you for giving me the chance to let Taya know I have everything under control now and should be able to see her soon."

"Good luck with whatever you're planning," Grayson said. "We'd best go. It's taken us a lot longer, than we expected, to find you." He turned to Summer. "Ready?"

She was more than ready. "Yes." Taking the flower from her pocket she dropped it on the ground, glancing towards Gale. "Good luck." She stood on the flower, taking them back to the clearing, the scent of strawberries swirling around them.

Grayson stared down at her, his arms around her waist. "There was no need to be jealous."

She wanted to argue his comment, but it was impossible. "Why would you say that?"

He grinned. "The wind picked up around us when Gale put her hand on my arm."

She pushed him away and turned to stride to the door.

He tugged her back. "I didn't say I didn't like it. Just that there's no need for you to feel that way."

She hadn't liked feeling that way. Had never felt like that before. "I don't normally act like that." Her eyes narrowed when she saw the look in his eyes change. "Stop planning whatever it is that you're planning."

"Are you sure?" He lowered his head, a breath away from her. "Absolutely sure?"

No, she wasn't. Her lips met his and she clung to him, breaking away from his embrace when the door of the cottage swung open.

"What took you so long?" Taya demanded.

Grayson handed over the letter and waited for Taya to read it before he spoke. "Are you satisfied that we've completed our part of the bargain?"

"Yes. You'll be on your way now?"

Grayson shook his head. "It's late and we're both

exhausted from looking for Gale. We were wondering if we could have something to eat, a wash and stay the night before we return home. The task you set us was far more complicated than you allowed us to believe."

"Then you leave. Don't expect to be arriving here whenever you feel like it. You want somewhere to stay in future, there's a deserted cottage a few miles that way." She pointed off to her right.

"Doesn't someone own it?" Summer asked.

"Been falling apart for decades. The wood Fae who lived there died and no one else moved in. Probably home to mice and spiders by now." Taya strode inside, leaving the door open.

"Surely people can't move into a place because it's been deserted for ages," Summer said.

"Things are different around here. If no one wants it then someone else will. It's probably deserted because no one knows it's there."

"One man's junk is another man's treasure?" Summer suggested.

Grayson chuckled. "Something like that." He gestured towards the open door. "We better go inside and find out what there is to eat before Taya changes her mind."

After they'd eaten the stew Taya served, Summer

and Grayson went out the backdoor, taking the lantern Taya offered them. She grumbled that she wasn't heating water for them and that they'd have to do it themselves, finding other things to complain about when they said they were fine.

Grayson stopped by the well and removed the wooden cap before heading to the tub. He put the wooden plug into the drain hole.

"What are you doing?" She'd expected him to return to the well, not stand near the tub frowning in concentration.

"Trying something." Water swirled through the air, splashing into the tub and spinning around until it slowly settled, reaching halfway to the top. The smell of rain hung in the air.

"Where did that come from?"

"The well." Grayson grinned at her. "Beats carrying buckets." He swirled his hand through it. "Check I haven't made it too hot." The smell of rain began to fade away.

She tested the water, leaving her hand trailing through the warmth as she continued to look at him. "How did you manage it?"

"I was practicing with water droplets on and off during the day. Mostly when you were sleeping. Shifting them around and making them move through the air. I wasn't sure I could do it with such a large amount of water."

"This is so confusing. I don't know how things work around here. Even the part about lying if you think it's the truth."

"I'll tell you two statements. Only one of them will be the truth. Repeat them back to me saying that it's what I think."

"How can you tell me a lie?"

"I'm not. I'm telling you that I'm about to state something that isn't true. So that means I'm not actually lying to you."

She slowly shook her head, more confused than ever. "Okay, tell me your statements."

"Remember, I'm about to tell you the opposite of what I think for one of them. First statement is that when I heard you were going to my aunt's birthday party I almost counted the days till you arrived." He plucked out a rose petal that had been caught in her hair. "The second statement is that you should cut your hair because it's too hard to take care of when it's long."

She repeated the statements back to him, starting each one with 'you think'. Neither felt any different to say. Not that it mattered. She knew which one was the truth. "You think I should cut my hair."

Grayson chuckled, picking one of the blooming roses. "Wrong." He scattered petals across the water. "Let me know when it's my turn."

She stared at his back until he stepped behind the rose bushes. He'd counted the days? That didn't seem possible. She trailed her hand through the water, petals clinging to her skin. He obviously liked her otherwise he wouldn't kiss her so often. She tried to say she didn't like him. The words wouldn't form. A smile formed instead. That was one thing she was sure of. Whether she had to visit him in this realm or the human one, she planned to see a lot more of Grayson.

She thought back over the time they'd spent together. It felt like months rather than days. Her smile turned into a grin. He'd counted the days. She would count the days when they were apart. Her grin disappeared. They weren't apart yet and she wasn't about to waste the time they did have together. Her smile returned as she brought the stone to her lips and asked if he could hear her.

His whispered reply came almost instantly. "It's my turn already?"

She laughed. A sound he would have heard both through the stone and drifting on the night air. She spoke against the stone. "Didn't you promise me more than buckets of warm water and a tub of stone surrounded by roses?"

Chapter Nineteen

The following morning Taya grudgingly fed them before they left her cottage, handing them a drawstring bag containing the clothes they'd worn when they'd arrived in the realms of the Fae. Holding hands they walked in the direction of the deserted cottage. It took them an hour to locate the cottage and Summer stared at the building, wondering if it was the vines, that trailed over it, that kept it from falling down.

"It's perfect."

She looked from Grayson to the ramshackle cottage. "Are you serious?"

"It's a renovator's delight."

"More like a renovator's nightmare."

"It can be fixed." Stepping forward, he opened the door, wincing when it leaned drunkenly, hanging from the bottom hinge.

Summer giggled. "Can it?"

Grayson brushed cobwebs from the doorway before he entered, stopping in the middle of the room. The floor was covered in dirt, leaves and droppings. "It might take a bit of time."

"I think that's an understatement. I thought you couldn't lie. At least not without saying it's a lie."

"I can't. I showed you that last night. I believe it's true, so I can say it even if you don't agree."

She frowned. "How can you believe that's true?"

"Do you want to know why you can't tell me 'no' about moving to the realms of the Fae? It's because you don't truly believe you want to return to the human realm. Part of you doesn't want to leave. Your magic can't tell the future. It can only know what you know. And you know that world isn't your home."

She avoided his comment, like he'd avoided her question. Last night they'd agreed not to talk about it until they'd returned home. She should have made the agreement magically binding. "Are you ready to go? There's nothing we can do here. Not without a building crew."

Grayson linked his fingers through hers, walking back outside, taking her with him. "Study this clearing. This is where we'll meet up if anything goes wrong. I don't think Taya wants to see us ever again."

She couldn't resist grinning as she remembered Taya's list of complaints that morning when she'd made them breakfast. "All right. We'll make this our meeting place, but I'm not staying here. I'd probably be carried off in the night by rodents. Either that or eaten alive by them." She scanned the area, focusing on all the things that made it unique, as well as the cottage that looked like it might fall down at any minute. "Okay. We can go now. I can return here if necessary."

"We should do something to make it seem like ours. So people know it isn't deserted."

"Are you crazy? There's nothing that can be done to this place to make it look less deserted." Spying some wildflowers, she gestured towards them. "Or did you think a handful of flowers was going to say home sweet home?"

Grinning, Grayson gathered up some of the flowers. "Great idea."

She slowly shook her head, fighting the urge to smile. "I think it needs a match. Burning it to the ground is the only way you'll be able to improve this place."

"Wait and see. One day it'll be better than Taya's." He strode inside and rummaged through the cupboards under the kitchen bench. The warped timber had more waves than the ocean.

Summer remained in the doorway. "What are you looking for?"

"A vase."

"I really doubt you're going to find one in there." She squealed when a mouse darted out of the cupboard, he'd been rummaging in, and ran towards her.

Grayson looked up from the next cupboard. "What's wrong?"

Unable to say the word 'nothing', heavily laden with sarcasm, she remained silent.

Grayson turned back to the cupboard. "Here we go." He stood up, holding out a glass, a large piece missing from the side. "A vase." He placed it on the bench, moving it until it was reasonably stable, and arranged the flowers in it.

"You think that makes it our place?"

"Yes. No one owns it, we've claimed it and put something that belongs to us here. It's ours."

"Like squatters."

"Yep." He dusted his hands off on his trousers. "Time to return to the human realm." He held out his hand.

"Time to go home," she corrected him.

"But whose home is it? Yours or your parents'?"

She placed her hand in his, unable to answer his question. "Can we travel from here directly to the national park?"

"We could, but do you know it well enough to take us there?"

She thought about it, shaking her head after a moment. She could probably take them to her bedroom, but there was no way she could explain that to her parents.

"The courtyard markets. We'll go back the same way we took Oliver." He paused a moment. "I didn't get the chance to say anything when we arrived back with him, Spencer interrupted. It felt different going through the exit. Normally we feel slightly disorientated. Everyone complains about it. But not this time. What did it feel like for you?"

"Nothing. Apart from that breeze. I didn't even know we'd changed realms."

"That's good. Should mean we won't forget this place when we turn twenty-one. The cursed exits obviously affect humans, not Fae."

"We are human."

"Humans don't have magic."

"We're Fae?"

"Not exactly. We'd probably be considered Demi Fae or something like that."

"Let's get out of here." She didn't allow herself to say the rest of the sentence, but the words rang in her head. Before I panic. She threw a strawberry flower on the floor and stepped on it, focusing on taking them to the courtyard markets. The world reformed around her, a Raptor standing directly in front of them.

Swearing, Grayson pulled her towards the closest alley. They didn't make it. His hand was dragged from hers and she spun to face the Raptor who struggled to capture Grayson.

Summer drew her sword, attacking. Grayson ended up sprawled on the ground when the Raptor shoved him away, drawing his own weapon. He met her blade before it could reach him. She could barely keep up with the return attacks, forced to defend, slowly being driven backwards. He was far more competent than any opponent she'd faced before. And he was aiming to wound or kill, not score points.

Two more Raptors dropped down out of the sky, their wings folding in as they reached the ground, tackling Grayson who'd gained his feet and was looking about for something to use as a weapon. Summer struggled to fend off the first Raptor, wanting to help Grayson, catching only glimpses of him being tied up. The two Raptors took to the sky, Grayson held between them.

"No!" She tried to run in the direction they took him.

The first Raptor slammed her against a wall. "I want my brother back." He'd drawn a dagger and held it against her throat. "Where is Lonan?"

"I don't know."

"Then you better find out before your friend loses his life." He stepped back, sheathing his weapons, his wings stretching out.

"Wait. I don't know who you are." She could guess, but didn't know for certain. "Or where to find you if I learn where Lonan is." She tried to keep herself from shaking, but it was impossible. They'd stolen Grayson and she had no idea how to find him.

"Perry. You already know where to find my castle. You stole your brother from there." He shot into the air, heading in the direction Grayson had been taken.

She slid down the wall, sitting on the uneven cobblestones, clutching the sword, the drawstring bag of clothes not far from her. A glance around the area showed no one looked in her direction, or even cared what had happened. She thought of the Fae who'd been stabbed on her first visit to the courtyard markets. No one had cared about helping him either. She rose shakily to her feet, trying to think what to do, as she grabbed the bag of clothes. She knew where they were taking him, had been there before. A shudder went through her as she remembered the glimpse she'd caught of the canyon the castle had been perched above.

This wasn't meant to happen. They were meant to be going home. Both of them. About to take Grayson's stone from her pocket, she saw two dark haired Fae walking towards her, daggers drawn. She was no match for them. Closing her hand, she formed a strawberry flower before tossing it on the ground and stepping on it, returning to the ramshackle cottage. The world reformed around her and she stumbled inside wanting to scream and beg someone to tell her Grayson wasn't gone. Her gaze was caught by the flowers Grayson had put on the bench only a short time earlier. Leaving the bag of clothes near the door, she crossed the room, stumbling over broken pieces of furniture. Before she had a chance to take one of the flowers from the glass, a sound had her spinning to face the back door.

"I thought the place was deserted."

Her grip tightened on her sword as she stared at the

narrow framed boy who appeared to be around her age. "You're human?"

He grinned, a friendly, reassuring grin. "Aren't you?" He came further into the cottage.

The grin didn't reassure her in the least. When her body ached a little as he came closer, her gaze was drawn to his hand. "You're wearing an iron ring?"

The grin faltered. "You're Fae? You don't look it. No pointy ears. Are you sure you're not human?"

She took a step back, running into the kitchen bench. "Once." How could it have been only a handful of days ago? Not even a week.

"Is something wrong?"

She tried to say 'no'. It was impossible. "I don't need your help. You can keep heading to wherever you were going."

"This was where I was going. There's a storm coming and this is the first shelter I've seen since the dark clouds began to form." He looked upwards. "Although I don't know how much shelter it's going to give us."

"This is my place. You weren't invited." It felt strange to say the words, knowing they had to be true.

"You're going to kick me out into an oncoming storm?"

Chapter Twenty

Summer could smell the rain and for a second thought it was Grayson arriving. Until droplets began to fall on the roof, some of them coming through to land on the floor. "Fine, but keep your iron away from me."

"I wear it to see through glamours."

"Through what?"

The boy lowered his backpack to the dusty floor, pulling out a small tarp to wrap it in. "How long have you been in the realms of the Fae?"

She shrugged, not wanting him to know how little time she'd spent here.

The boy examined a table that was on its side and against a wall. "The Fae can use a glamour to hide what they are from humans. Wearing iron, or having magic, lets you see through it." He gestured towards the table. "Want to help me stand this up? If the rain gets too heavy we can sit under it and keep dry."

After sheathing the sword, she helped him to right the table and move it away from the wall. A glance around showed there were no chairs, although some of the broken bits of furniture might once have been chairs.

On the wall where the table had been was a fireplace. The boy put pieces of broken furniture in it, setting about building a fire that he left unlit.

"What are you doing?" She remained well back, not wanting to get too close to his ring.

"In case the rain lasts all day and we're stuck here." He eyed the space under the table and in front of the fire. "A pity we don't have a broom."

She sighed. He obviously wasn't going away until the rain stopped. "Out of the way and I'll clean it." At least she hoped she could. Once he stood behind her, she sent a breeze skimming across the floor, directing the mess out the back door. A few times she had to edge the wind back around to collect something that had been left behind, making the wind encircle it so the dust and dirt wasn't scattered everywhere.

"That's pretty handy." The boy grinned at her. "It'd make drying clothes quicker." He brought his backpack over to the table and stowed it underneath, taking out a folded piece of paper.

"What are you doing?"

He spread a hand drawn map out on the table. "Marking in this location."

"No."

The boy stared at her. "Why not? There's no maps of this realm and large sections of it are unexplored."

"Maybe some people would prefer not to be on any map or easily found."

"I didn't think about that. Are you hiding?"

She thought about his question for a moment, particularly since she knew she couldn't say no. "I'm waiting for someone." Why hadn't Grayson called her using the flower?

The boy held out his hand, the one without the iron ring. "What's your name? I'm-"

"I already know who you are. You're an intruder." She didn't need anyone else to worry about.

The boy laughed. "I suppose I am. Are you sure you're not hiding?"

She turned her back on him, striding to the front door and looking out at the light rain. It'd be mean to send him out in it. She sighed again. Why hadn't Grayson contacted her? Drawing the stone from her pocket, she whispered against it, asking him if he could hear her. There was no reply. She spoke several more times, wanting to know where he was. The only sounds she could hear were that of the falling rain and the steady drips behind her where it leaked through the roof in numerous places. Her hand tightened over the stone. Why wouldn't Grayson answer her?

"Do you want something to eat? I doubt you'll want to eat what's in your cupboards."

She faced the boy to stare at the apple he held out. She shook her head. It wasn't that long since she'd eaten at Taya's place. Her and Grayson. She went back to staring outside, frequently whispering against the stone. Eventually she whispered, "If I don't hear from you soon, I'm coming after you." Her stomach did a long slow turn as she tried not to think about when they'd rescued her brother. That hadn't worked out so well. At least not at first.

"You're not very talkative, are you?"

She looked over her shoulder. The boy was lying under the table, using his backpack as a pillow. Maybe if she didn't answer him he'd stop trying to talk to her. She returned to staring outside. The rain was getting heavier, the sound of the drips behind her becoming louder. A glance at the drawstring bag showed it was in a dry location. Not that there were many of them. Her gaze was drawn to the numerous leaks. She didn't have a bucket to catch them. Or a couple of dozen buckets. Thinking of buckets made her think of the well, which in turn led to thoughts of last night.

Pain arrowed through her. She couldn't lose Grayson. That was it. She was going after him. She raised the stone to her lips. "I'm coming after you." She closed her hand, opening it seconds later to reveal a strawberry flower. Tipping it off her hand she watched as it drifted to the ground.

"No."

For a second she thought the boy had spoken. She turned around to look at him. His eyes were closed and he continued to lie beneath the table.

"Don't follow me."

She closed her eyes. It had been Grayson, his voice like a whisper on the breeze. Facing outside, she spoke against the stone. "Why didn't you answer me?"

"It's hard to get something out of your pocket when your hands are tied behind your back."

"I'll come and get you."

"Aren't you listening? I said no."

"Why not?" There was a lengthy pause and she began to wonder if he'd answer. "Are you trying to figure out how to lie to me?" Laughter filled the air around her. "Tell me the truth, Grayson. Or I'm coming after you." Again there was a lengthy silence.

"You know those tall rock pillars you see in canyons?"

"Not personally."

"I didn't either until today."

Her breath stopped halfway through breathing in. She tried to speak, but all she could do was stand in the doorway with her mouth hanging open.

"What are you planning?"

Again she tried to speak. Not a single sound. She stared at the strawberry flower lying on the ground, raindrops splashing mud onto it.

"Are you okay?"

She sat down, dampness seeping into her trousers. "Where exactly are you?"

"On top of one of those rock pillars. It's probably about a metre in diameter. You can't land on top of it. You'd probably fall off. It's a long way to the canyon floor."

She picked up the flower, watching a streak of mud slide across a petal. "You'll have to use your magic to get out of there."

"Do you think I haven't tried? I'm chained here. There's a stake driven into the ground and a chain attached to it, the end locked around my ankle. I tried to use magic to get out of here. It didn't work. Either I'm not that good at it or the chain stops me from leaving."

There was an ache at the back of her throat and she looked up to see if she was under one of the many holes in the ceiling. She wasn't. Wiping the back of her hand across her face, she realised it was tears dampening her cheeks. "I don't know how to find Lonan."

"Ask around the Fringes. Someone has to know. I should have left the money with you." Grayson was silent a moment. "You can use your earrings for trade. They're valuable."

She wanted to tell him she'd rescue him. But she couldn't. The words froze in her throat. "I'll let you know when I find out anything."

"Be careful."

"You too." She slipped the stone back in her pocket as she stood up.

"Are you going somewhere?"

She faced the boy, nodding. "The Fringes."

His gaze momentarily rested on the flower she held. "You going to use magic to get there?"

Again she nodded.

"Can you take me with you?"

"No."

"Why not?"

It took her a moment to decide it wasn't worth the effort of trying to avoid the truth. "You were almost correct before. I'm not hiding, but I am being hunted. You don't want to be associated with me or your life could be in danger."

"Do you need any help?"

"Did you hear what I said?"

The boy grinned. "Yeah. It wouldn't be the first time I've helped someone who was being hunted. So do you want help?"

She was tempted. More than tempted. "No." Dropping the flower on the ground, she stepped on it, taking herself to the Fringes, arriving out the front of the doctor's house. It wasn't raining here so she called up a breeze to dry herself before knocking on the door.

The doctor opened the door, remaining in the doorway. "What do you want?"

"Information."

"It better not be to do with Lonan. I'm not getting mixed up in that. No one sane would want to."

"Getting mixed up in what?"

The doctor pointed a finger at her. "You think to trick something out of me that way?"

"It isn't a trick. I don't know what's going on."

The doctor tried to close the door.

She put her hand against the timber. "Wait. You owe us. Perry has Grayson."

"Then you better find his brother for him. He's not a patient man."

"I don't know how. I don't even know who has him."

"Skah."

"That name means nothing to me." She kept her hand pressed against the door, not letting him close it.

"The name will mean something to Perry." The doctor finally managed to shut the door.

She stared at the timber, tempted to bang on it again. She doubted he'd answer. Was that enough information for Perry to let her have Grayson? Not knowing what else to do, she formed a flower in her hand and let it drift to the cobblestones. He'd said she knew where to find him. The only place she could safely take herself was to his dungeon. It better not be a trap. Bringing an image of the place to mind, she stepped on the flower, the scent of strawberries clung to her when the world reformed and she found herself in Perry's dungeon.

A Raptor drew his sword, warily watching her. "You the girl Perry is waiting for?" He glanced around the dungeon. "Where's his brother? Where's Lonan?"

"I need to talk to Perry."

"Are you sure you want to see him when you don't have his brother with you?"

Not really, but she couldn't think of anything else to do. "Take me to him."

"Go ahead of me." The Raptor kept his sword drawn, indicating the direction Summer should take.

She walked ahead, frequently glancing over her shoulder, uncomfortable with a drawn sword at her back. She was tempted to draw her own, but guessed he'd take it the wrong way and attack. They eventually reached a room where Perry sat playing chess with another Raptor, the table set beside a window that looked out over a dizzying drop. Summer averted her gaze, focusing on Perry.

"Where's my brother?"

"I learned that Skah has him."

"Where is he keeping him? I doubt it'd be at his castle. That'd be too close to Chenoa."

She was about to ask who Chenoa was, when she recalled Lonan warning that taking his magic wouldn't keep him away from her. Nor would her father. "Skah is Chenoa's father?"

"You aren't very interested in keeping your friend alive, are you?" He gestured towards the window.

She automatically looked, catching a glimpse of a figure sitting on the top of a rock spire before she dragged her gaze away, trying to fight the light-headedness and the need to throw up. "I don't know where Skah lives. How can I find out where he's taken Lonan?"

Perry turned to the Raptor who continued to hold his sword. "Take her out the front and point her in the right direction."

Staying to argue would have been pointless. She clearly heard the dismissal in his tone. The Raptor gestured for her to go ahead. She walked through the castle until they reached the front entrance, stopping at the top of an elaborate staircase.

The Raptor pointed off to his left. "Skah's castle is that way. A couple of hours flight from here."

"I can't fly."

"Then you better get started. Walking isn't the quickest way of getting around." He returned inside.

Chapter Twenty-One

Summer stared at the two Raptors who guarded the entrance. They weren't about to let her back inside. And she doubted they'd answer any of the many questions she had. Walking down the steps she couldn't stop thinking about Grayson. He wasn't far from her. On the other side of the castle. But he might as well be in another realm. She couldn't face a small drop let alone the extremely deep one she'd caught a glimpse of.

Reaching the bottom of the steps she looked between both directions. Grayson and Skah. Neither option was appealing. Her gaze returned to the castle. "This is ridiculous," she muttered. She strode around the side of the castle, determined to face the canyon. There was no reason why she should be terrified of heights. None at all. She had to do this. There was no other way to help Grayson.

Her determination brought her to the edge of the cliff where she swayed on her feet, the world fading around the edges as she tried not to pass out. Across from her she could see Grayson, a tiny figure who seemed to be growing smaller by the second. Then she was tumbling, plunging head first towards the floor of the canyon. She opened her mouth to scream. The wind rushed at her, tearing all sound from her. Even though she knew it was a waste of time, she put out her hands to break her fall. A gust of wind came up to meet her, the scent of strawberries swirling around her. She landed face first in the dirt, softly, the air breaking her fall.

She shook so hard that she couldn't move for a couple of minutes. Eventually she rolled over onto her back to face the sky. It was a long way above, rock pillars towering over her. She'd survived the fall. Her heart thudded loudly, letting her know she was alive. Sitting up, she looked around, the dust having settled. "Alive." The word was a whisper, filled with wonder and disbelief. "I'm alive." She spoke slightly louder as she stood up, her legs shaky. Disbelief rolled through her. It shouldn't have been possible.

Patting down her body she couldn't find a single bruise let alone a broken limb. Her head spun, but not with dizziness. She slowly turned around, trying to comprehend everything. "I'm alive." Tilting her head back she looked up to the top of the cliff. Her gaze travelled down the full length of it until it reached the ground. Her stomach slowly turned. Not too bad. She wasn't light headed and she didn't feel like losing her breakfast. At least not yet.

Her gaze rose to the top of the cliff again. She didn't have to be afraid of falling. Frowning, she tried to catch hold of an image of falling off a balcony, greenery coming up to meet her. Had that happened? Had she fallen once, a long time ago? She pulled up the leg of her trousers and sat on the ground to stare at the faint white line that went along the side of her leg, barely noticeable these days. Running a finger over it, she thought of what she always told people when they asked her what had happened. A stick. One she couldn't remember. She'd been giving that answer for so many years it was now an automatic response, no thought behind it at all. And no remembrance of the incident that had caused the scar. Again she saw the image of falling off a balcony.

Lowering the leg of her trousers, she rose to her feet. There was no one here to give her any answers. She faced the canyon. The only person here, other than herself, needed her help to escape. She looked upwards once more, reassured when there was no light-headedness, only the slow turn of her stomach. She could do this. She had to.

Taking out the stone, she pressed it to her lips. "Can you hear me?"

He didn't reply immediately. "Have you found Lonan?"

"Stand on the edge of the pillar and make sure there's as much space as possible in front of you."

"No. You're not coming here. You'll pass out and fall over the edge. A drop like that would kill you."

"It didn't."

"It-" He broke off, silent for a moment. "Where are you?"

"On the floor of the canyon."

"What happened?"

She smiled at the hesitant tone of his voice. "I'll tell you once you're off that pillar. Are you ready for me?"

"Don't do this. Don't take the risk."

"I can do it." She smiled. "You know I can't lie." When he didn't speak, she asked, "Are you ready?"

"Be careful."

"I will. Are you ready?"

"Yes."

Her stomach did another slow turn. She waited a moment to see if she grew dizzy or wanted to throw up. Nothing else happened. After slipping the rock into her pocket she used a strawberry flower to take her to Grayson, focusing on the image of his eyes.

His arms wrapped around her and his lips pressed against hers. "You're crazy." He kissed her again. "Insane."

She turned her head when he would have kissed her once more. "We have to get out of here. They can see you from the castle." She bent to look at the stake in the ground, a length of rope lying nearby looking like rats had chewed through it.

"Once I finished using the stake to saw through the rope around my wrists I tried to wash the dirt away with water from the air. There isn't a lot of moisture around here. It's too dry and dusty."

A channel had been washed away, but it was only a few centimetres deep. "I'll use the wind. It's probably what shaped this canyon over the years." Standing, she caught the nearest breeze and arrowed it towards the stake. Dust flew away from it, swirling on the breeze. She gathered more winds, forcing them together and continuing to direct them at the ground around the stake.

"We've got a problem."

She didn't have time to look. It took all her concentration to wear away the dirt.

"Four Raptors flying towards us and they have crossbows."

This time when her stomach lurched she felt a little light headed. Being shot was going to be a lot more painful than falling off a cliff.

"Summer. Go." Grayson tugged on the stake. It remained in place.

She drew in more wind. The ones she held fought against her as she kept them biting into the dirt. Movement caught her attention and she turned to see a bolt coming directly towards her. The winds twisted around in front of them, the bolt thrown back when it came into contact with the winds. She flung the winds towards the Raptors and they spiralled away to avoid them.

"The stake is nearly out. I felt it move a fraction."

She dragged the winds back, forcing them at the ground once more. The stake came out of the ground and she flung the winds at the Raptors who were flying towards them again, crossbows once more aimed in their direction.

Grayson gathered the chain into loops and grabbed hold of Summer. "Leave. Now. They're coming back."

She threw down the flower she'd formed and stepped on it, picturing the doctor's place. It took a few seconds to concentrate with the Raptors bearing down on them. A handful of wind came too, swirling down the street when they arrived. She patted Grayson over like she'd done to herself earlier. "You're okay? You're not hurt?" Her heart thudded wildly and her body was tense, waiting for the attack that didn't come.

"I'm fine." He captured one of her hands. "Why did you bring us here? You should have taken us to our place."

She shook her head. "We have to go home. It's not safe here."

His hand tightened on hers. "We'll make it safe."

"How?"

"Rescue Lonan."

This time when her stomach slowly turned she felt like she might throw up. "We can't." She shook her head, backing away from him.

He followed, the chain rattling, his hand holding hers. "We can. I know we can."

"No, we can't."

"We can do anything. Didn't you stand on top of a rock pillar without a problem?"

"That was different." She briefly explained falling off the cliff and the vague memory she'd had of the balcony.

"We'll make this different too. Perry wants his brother back. After that, if anything else happens to him, he's not our problem. Just one more thing to do and then we can return to the human world."

The doctor flung open his door before Summer could continue to argue. "Will you stop turning up on my doorstep? I don't need the kind of trouble you bring."

"Can you get this chain off my leg?" The chain rattled when Grayson raised the hand that held it.

"Find a blacksmith." The doctor slammed the door shut.

"Where are we going to find one of them?" She stared at the door, wondering if she should knock on it and ask. "Better yet. Keep it on and we can say you were chained up when we get home."

"The courtyard marketplace." He met her gaze. "You can go home if you want. I can show you where the exit is."

She wanted to tell him he was crazy, that they couldn't go after Lonan. The words wouldn't form. Apparently she was as crazy as him. She wasn't tempted to leave him behind. Sighing, she looked in the direction of the courtyard marketplace. "You better not get us killed."

"I have no plans to." Grayson started forward, the chain rattling at each step.

She fell in beside him, unable to resist giggling.

"What's funny?"

"You look too healthy to be rattling chains."

"I was worried earlier that I wouldn't remain healthy."

The urge to giggle disappeared. "So was I." She slipped her hand in his. "We really should go home before something else happens." She tried to put some effort in the words, but they lacked conviction. They should go home, but it looked like she wasn't any more interested in leaving things undone than he was.

"We can't leave Lonan caught because we stole his magic. We're going to make it safe to return here."

She fell silent, knowing he'd go through with it even if he had to do it alone. She wasn't about to let him do that. Fear of losing him arrowed through her, not as bad as it had been earlier. Somehow they had to find a way to get Perry to stop hunting them. Otherwise Grayson wouldn't be safe here. Neither of them would. The last thought nearly made her stop walking. Neither of them? Before she could figure out if she was thinking of staying, they reached the blacksmith.

Grayson held up the chain. "Can you remove this?"

"What will you pay me?" The blacksmith crossed his arms over his chest, a leather apron stretched over his front.

"The chain?" Summer tried not to focus on his bottom incisors that protruded over his top lip, claiming him something other than human.

"The entire chain?"

She had no idea what to offer. "Yes."

The blacksmith grinned. "Gladly."

"We've overpaid you, haven't we?" His grin had been too wide and there was a definite gleam in his eyes. She was pretty sure she was right.

"The bargain has been struck."

"I know. I'm not trying to get out of it, I'm curious."

"About four times too much." The blacksmith chuckled. "Come over here, lad, and I'll remove it for you."

Summer watched as the chain was removed, the blacksmith checking out his payment as they headed back the way they'd come. "How are we going to find Lonan?"

"Do you remember what he looks like?"

She stopped abruptly. "We are not doing that again. We're not that-" She broke off, unable to say the word 'crazy'. Apparently they were crazy and she completely believed it.

"We are doing that. Do you remember what he looks like?"

Chapter Twenty-Two

Summer sighed heavily. How had she gone from almost normal, other than her fear of heights, to crazy enough to think she could rescue people and use magic in a way that most sane people avoided? She looked away from Grayson, not sure if she should tell him it was a little hard to forget someone who wanted to kill you.

"Well?"

"Yes." She muttered the word, half hoping he wouldn't hear it clearly.

"Good."

"Not the word I would have used."

Grayson chuckled. "It will be. Once we've returned Lonan to his brother and no one wants to kill us anymore."

She thought of the chain they'd given to the blacksmith. They could have used it to explain what had happened to them. "What are we going to tell out parents?"

"Nothing."

"But–"

"Have you forgotten we can't lie?"

"Oh."

Grayson grinned. "Yeah, exactly. Say that there's nothing you can tell them. Let them take that how they will."

"Life is going to be impossible when I can't lie."

"Do you tend to lie often?"

"Nothing major. Well, it kind of is, but it's not bad. I have a friend with low self-esteem. If I can't tell a few white lies her self-esteem is going to get dramatically lower."

"Bend the truth. The Fae manage to do it very well."

"I have no idea how to do that."

"We could stay here longer and I could teach you."

"Our parents must be frantic. We have to go back."

"Yeah."

"Where are we going?"

"To see the doctor. I need more magic. What I have isn't enough."

She stopped, holding out her hand, magic forming in it. "Why didn't you say?"

"I can't take that. We can't run you short either."

"I had trouble trying to stand a couple of metres away from a boy with an iron ring."

Grayson held out his hand. "What boy?"

She tipped the magic into his palm and watched as it sunk in. "He turned up at our place while I was waiting for you to answer me."

Grayson smiled.

"What are you looking at me like that for?"

"Our place." The smile widened into a grin. "Even you admit it."

"Are we going to rescue Lonan or stand around talking?"

Grayson tugged her close, wrapping an arm around her waist. "There are other things I'd rather be doing, but we need to rescue Lonan." He lightly brushed his lips across hers. "We'll take him to his brother's castle."

"Okay." She tightened her hand into a fist, dreading finding out where Lonan was held. "Are you ready?"

"Yes."

She let the flower fall to the ground beside her foot, stepping on it as she brought an image of Lonan to mind. The world shimmered and reformed as pitch-blackness.

"What are you doing here?" Lonan demanded.

The room slowly brightened for her and she noticed the scent of strawberries. "We've come to get you out of here."

Lonan tugged his leg, a chain keeping him from moving far from the wall. "Then you better have brought something to remove this."

Grayson slowly turned on the spot. "We should have brought a lantern with us."

"What's with you people and chains?" Summer demanded.

"It keeps people from escaping," Lonan said dryly.

"I'll bring the blacksmith back." She reached for Grayson's hand, not wanting to leave him with Lonan.

The Raptor grabbed Grayson's other hand, dragging him closer. "He stays with me."

Summer wanted to argue. She kept quiet when Grayson shook his head. "I won't be long." She stared at Grayson a moment before she returned to collect the blacksmith, arriving nearby.

"Back again already? You better not be wanting the chain. A deal is a deal."

She shook her head, explaining what she needed.

"And what will be my payment this time?'

"Another chain?" She couldn't resist grinning.

The blacksmith chuckled. "You sure no one will catch us? I don't want to go against any Raptors. Especially not Skah. Vindictive doesn't come close to describing him. On the other hand you can't fault how loyal he is to those he believes deserves it."

"Can't you tell him I kidnapped you?"

"How about you give me my alibi."

"What do you mean?"

"A threat I can tell him you made if we're caught."

"Oh." She remembered how Grayson had been able to lie when he'd told her he would. "Which tools will you need?"

"Only that one." He pointed to the one he'd need.

She picked up the tool and shoved it at him so he was forced to take it. Throwing a flower on the ground, she grabbed his hand a second before she stepped on it, taking him back to the dungeon with her. A glance around showed no one else had entered the dungeon while she'd been gone. "Now you've been kidnapped."

"That's all very well," the blacksmith said, "but I can't see in the dark. I'm not a full blood Troll."

"Are you all useless?" Lonan demanded.

"I'd do it if I could see anything," Grayson said.

"Hand it here." Lonan took the tool from the blacksmith and cut the chain from his ankle.

"It needs to be cut from the wall too." Summer took the tool from Lonan once he was done and handed the chain and tool to the blacksmith. "I won't be long." She took hold of the blacksmith's hand and returned him to the courtyard marketplace. "Thank you."

The blacksmith held up the chain. "Normally the one who is kidnapped pays the ransom. Glad to see you do things the other way around." He grinned. "Good luck. You're going to need it getting mixed up with Raptors. Make sure you don't trust a word they say. Even though they can't lie somehow nearly every word they utter happens to be one."

"Thanks." She returned to the dungeon, swaying slightly, leaning against Grayson.

"You okay?" Grayson wrapped an arm around her waist.

She didn't bother answering, knowing she wouldn't be able to say yes. Turning to Lonan, she held out a hand. "Time to return you to your brother."

"I'm not leaving here without Chenoa. Her father isn't going to keep us apart. Take me outside."

"I can't. I don't know what this place looks like."

"How did you get in here?"

Worried she shouldn't be telling him, she turned to

Grayson who half shrugged at her movement against him. It wasn't much in the way of advice, but he hadn't said no. "I pictured you."

"I thought humans were more cautious than that." Lonan laughed, a sound more like a screech. "Then you can picture the woman I love since you have no care for your safety." He took a small portrait from a pocket.

Summer stared at it, examining the Raptor. Her feathers were white, the tops of some of them tinged with grey. Her face wasn't as sharp as Lonan's. It was softer and more rounded.

"Can you take me to her?" Lonan took the painting back. "Would you leave behind someone you love? Someone you can't live without?"

She was sick of being hunted. "If I do this, take you to Chenoa, you and your family are to never come after us again for any reason."

Grayson spoke before Lonan could. "That includes sending others after us, causing us harm in any way, having us imprisoned or visiting any kind of misfortune on us. Nor can you use anyone we care for to strike back at us in any of the already mentioned ways. The bargain will be sealed with magic and be valid regardless of the situation we find Chenoa in. Even if she's surrounded by an army. And regardless of any future consequences caused by your or our actions regarding this matter."

Lonan grinned. "My magic has returned enough that I'd be able to escape an army and take her with me. Will we arrive as close to her as you arrived to me?'

"Yes. I know no other way of doing it."

"Then we have a bargain." Lonan held out a hand to Summer, taking hold of Grayson's hand with the other.

When she took it, the dungeon filled with the scent of magic from the three of them. She tried to let go of his hand.

Lonan kept hold of her hand, only releasing Grayson's. "We will go now."

She nodded, forming a flower and letting it drift to the floor. She closed her eyes, bringing to mind the Raptor with the grey tipped white feathers as she slid her arm around Grayson's waist. Opening her eyes, she stepped on the flower, the dungeon shimmering out of focus, the next destination not coming into focus as it should. It took her a few seconds to realise it was because of how light headed she was, the edges of her vision darkening.

Lonan let go of her hand to grab hold of the Raptor in front of him. "I told you nothing would keep us apart." He shot into the sky, taking Chenoa with him, her scream trailing behind them to where they stood in an open courtyard, pots filled with succulents around the edges, a raised pond in the middle.

Raptors flew down around them, others giving chase. A Raptor with pure white feathers landed. His face had the rounded look of Chenoa's, but there was no softness in either his face or his expression.

"You will both die for letting Lonan steal my daughter again."

"Now would be a good time to get us out of here," Grayson said softly.

She tried to form a flower in her closed hand. Nothing happened. "He told us you were keeping them apart. That he loved her."

"Then he didn't tell you the full truth. I was keeping them apart because he kidnapped her when she turned him down."

A flower finally formed and she let it drift to the ground, leaning into Grayson's arm he had around her. "Don't let me fall." She stepped on the flower, taking them to their place, blackness rushing in on her.

She woke to the flickering light of a fire. Turning her head she saw she was in front of the fireplace at the ramshackle cottage. When she struggled to sit up, she felt arms around her, helping.

"You should have told me you were close to passing out," Grayson said.

"I didn't know we'd have to leave again so soon."

"You shouldn't have given me any magic."

She pressed her fingers against his lips. "I don't think it would have made a difference." She drew away from him. "Is the boy here?"

"He's gone. He left you a letter."

"What does it say?"

"I don't know. It was addressed to you." He reached past her to pick up a folded piece of paper.

Chapter Twenty-Three

Summer stared at the paper, the bright white of the A4 seeming out of place in this realm. Across the front he'd written 'To the girl who was once human'. She smiled, taking the letter from Grayson and opening it up. 'Thank you for your grudging hospitality. I brought in firewood to replace what I used when I cooked my lunch and stacked a bit at the back door. Don't worry, your home is safe from being added to any map of my making. You made a good point. In future I'll check to see if it's safe to add any single dwellings I come across. From The Intruder.' She handed the letter to Grayson so he could read it.

After he'd finished, he asked a few questions, particularly about the map. He folded the letter and handed it back to her. "It's good he'll keep those locations safe in future. Many of those living off by themselves do so for a reason." He paused a moment. "Are you hungry?"

"Starving. What time is it?"

"Nearly morning."

"Where did you get food from? You didn't hassle Taya, did you?'

"No. I cleaned up outside a bit so I wouldn't disturb you and found a root cellar. There was nothing edible in there, but I did find a couple of pots I cleaned up using water from the well out the back."

"Where did you find the food to put in the pots?"

"There used to be a vegetable garden by the well. It's run wild and many of the plants have grown beyond their original area so it was a bit like a treasure hunt finding enough vegetables for a meal."

When he started to move away, she took hold of his hand. "We have to go back. Or at least I do."

"I know."

"But we need to rescue Chenoa first."

Grayson grinned. "Just one more thing?"

A wry smile formed. "Let's hope it is only one."

"I'll get you something to eat and we'll work on a plan. Something better than appearing in front of her and stealing her from wherever Lonan has stashed her. He'll be expecting that."

"I'll go."

"No." He held up his hand when she went to argue. "Food and then we'll discuss it."

Her stomach rumbled and she smiled. "Okay. Food first."

It didn't take them long to eat and then they returned to arguing over what to do. Summer was adamant she could transport herself to Chenoa and, even if it was on the edge of a cliff, she'd survive.

"You're not taking that chance. There could be other things."

She stared at him, looking at the space between them. "He thinks I always arrive up close. What if I learn not to?"

"No."

She glared at him. "Then tell me what we can do instead of constantly saying 'no'. Give me a plan."

Grayson looked towards the fire, which had died down low. "I don't have a plan." He faced her again. "But you're not getting yourself killed. That isn't acceptable."

"I'm terrified of losing you too." She reached for him, holding him as tightly as he currently held her. "But we have to do this or we'll have Skah after us. I think he'll be a more dangerous enemy than Lonan."

"I know." He drew away from her so he could meet her gaze. "You don't know if you can travel to someone and arrive at a distance. You might not be able to."

"We'll test it."

They stepped out the front door to find the sky was turning grey with early morning light. Summer made Grayson go out the back of the cottage to an area she hadn't seen. It took her several minutes to figure out what she should do. She smiled when she heard his voice on the air beside her. Instead of replying, she formed a flower and dropped it onto the ground, travelling to Grayson. She eyed the distance between them. There had to be at least five metres. "It worked."

"What did you do?"

"Pictured your eyes that far from me, instead of up close like I normally do."

"Only my eyes?"

She shrugged. "I like your eyes. They tell me things." She chuckled. "Like now. You look like you're planning mischief."

He strode towards her. "Not exactly what I had in mind, but close enough." He kissed her, holding her tightly. When he drew back, he stared at her for a moment. "Be careful."

"Of course I will."

"We need to decide where we'll take her once we

get her away from where she's being held. We're not bringing her back here. I don't want anyone knowing this is our place."

"The doctor won't want us turning up on his doorstep." She couldn't resist smiling at the way he'd slammed the door. He'd get over it once no one was after them.

"The courtyard markets are too dangerous. If Lonan's people are there they'll steal her back. If Skah's are there they'll probably shoot us on sight. We need somewhere that we can negotiate with her."

She thought of all the different places she knew in this realm. "The grate where we escaped Lonan."

"That'll work." He held both her hands. "Come back as soon as you find a location we can both be in."

"Unless it's an easy rescue."

"Not even then. We both need to be there to talk to her. So we can make a binding agreement between all of us."

"Okay. I'll be back soon." She formed a flower and crushed it under her foot, picturing Chenoa, but at a distance. She barely managed to get a glimpse of Chenoa, tied to a wall, standing on a narrow ledge, the ground in front of her covered in spikes and animal traps with sharp jaws ready to snap shut at the slightest pressure, before she was plummeting down. Dragging air towards herself to use as a cushion, she struggled to find a single breeze. She hit shallow water, her arms flailing as she surfaced in a tangle of weeds when she tried to stand. A glance around the area showed she was in a cave, an underground stream winding its way through the middle, crocodiles slipping into the water from the edges of the bank.

Fear rushed through her and her stomach somersaulted as she tried to get out of the water. There appeared to be nowhere to go. Around her more crocodiles splashed into the waist deep water and she backed up until she ran into the cave wall that led to where Chenoa was held captive. Her plan wasn't going well and she was glad Grayson wasn't with her. She tried to take a deep breath. It was impossible. It was as uneven as her heartbeat.

Facing the rock wall, trying not to think of the crocodiles, she noticed the surface of it was rough and tried to climb up it. Hand and foot holds were narrow and her grip slipped several times. Partway up, she found a slightly larger handhold and clung to it as she surveyed the cave. At this height she was able to see a ledge across from her that she could travel to if she could manage to step on a flower. Now wasn't the time to learn how to crush it with her hand. The ledge wasn't wide enough for any errors.

It took nearly a minute to make a flower form and during that time she heard Grayson ask why she was taking so long. There was no way she could take the stone from her pocket and answer him. Placing the flower on the ledge she clung to, she tried to go higher. Her foot slipped and fear raced through her, causing her heart rate to increase. Below several crocodiles snapped at each other. She couldn't manage to go anywhere. Her stomach did a slow turn, but she didn't feel the slightest bit dizzy. Taking a deep breath, she tried to slow the beat of her heart. It remained fast, but the fear receded slightly. She could do this. It wasn't as bad as plummeting off a cliff.

She examined the spot across from her. If she travelled there then went back for Grayson and returned, she might be pushing herself too much. It made more sense to collect Grayson first. If she could stand on her flower.

Hoping the flower remained on the ledge, she tried to climb higher. This time when her grip slipped, she slid down, grabbing at handholds as she passed them. She continued to slide, her heart racing and her breath coming in gasps as the crocodiles jumped up at her. The snapping sound had her struggling to slow her descent. Drawing air from around the area, she pushed it beneath her feet. There was another snap below her as she came to a stop, sharp teeth closing on nothing.

Leaning back against the wall, she held onto the air as she reached for a handhold. Not finding one, she ran her hand across the wall. Where were they? Another snap below had a shiver travelling through her. Hearing Grayson speak again nearly broke her concentration and the air beneath her feet gave way a fraction.

"Answer me or I'm coming after you."

Her fingers finally found a handhold and she pulled herself up, aiming for the spot where she'd left the flower. Using the air to help, she crept up the wall, finally pressing her foot down on the flower and travelling back to Grayson, landing in a heap at his feet.

He crouched in front of her, drawing her up to a sitting position. "What happened?"

She thought of and discarded several words. "Don't panic."

"Saying that almost guarantees someone is going to panic."

"There were crocodiles."

"What!"

She closed her eyes and lowered her head to rest the top of it against his chest. "He was expecting us. Expecting me."

"Tell me."

It was a minute before she could lift her head and meet his gaze. "Only another Raptor can get her out of there." She described the location for him, waiting for him to comment once she'd finished. When he didn't, she spoke again. "We can't go to her father. He's likely to kill us on sight."

"How tall are the spikes? What if we sent something over there to set off the traps? Would there be enough space then?"

"I don't know."

"We'll find a handful of rocks and take them with us."

"There were some on the banks with the crocodiles."

"Will you be able to get them?"

"If I can't lift them from their location with air then I won't be able to get them across the cave to set off the traps."

Grayson stood, drawing her up with him, keeping hold of one of her hands. "Let's go."

Chapter Twenty-Four

Summer wanted to tell Grayson to wait, that she wasn't ready. But how long would Lonan leave Chenoa where she was? What if he took her somewhere worse? "Okay." She formed a flower, dropping it to the ground and stepping on it, taking them to the spot she'd chosen while trying to avoid being eaten alive by a crocodile.

The ledge was narrower than she'd thought and she pressed herself against the wall when her foot slipped over the edge.

Grayson pressed himself against the wall next to her, his hand tightening on hers. "You fell down there?"

She looked to where he nodded, the crocodiles fighting over a prey that was no longer there. Not wanting to focus on her close call, she gestured towards Chenoa who remained tied to a wall, a gag tight around her mouth. Wanting to let the woman know she'd be rescued, she sent her voice on the air. "I'm sorry. We didn't know Lonan planned to kidnap you. We'll set you free."

Chenoa shook her head, fear in her eyes.

"I'll set off the traps from here." Again she sent her voice on the air.

Chenoa continued to shake her head.

"What do you think is wrong?" Summer asked.

"I don't know, but we have to do something. We can't leave her there. Send a rock over and set off one of the traps along the edge."

Choosing a rock from the bank, she gathered up the air, turning it into a focused breeze. The rock lifted, tumbling back to the bank. This time she made a pocket with the breeze, forcing the rock to remain in the middle as she pushed it towards the ledge Chenoa was on. The woman continued to shake her head, trying to talk past the gag, struggling against the ropes.

The rock landed on one of the animal traps and it snapped shut, an arrow flying towards Chenoa from one of the side walls. Summer had been about to release the breeze, but forced it upwards, intercepting the arrow before it struck the woman. Summer began to shake and sagged against Grayson, who put an arm around her, holding her tight.

"I'm sorry." She sent the words to Chenoa, who nodded, tears running down her cheeks to soak into the gag. "What are we going to do?" She faced Grayson in the hope that Chenoa couldn't figure out what she was saying. They were meant to be rescuing her, not getting her killed.

"You were right. Only another Raptor can save her."

She didn't want to be right. "We don't know another Raptor. Not one we can ask for help."

"Go to her father. That thing you did with the air to deflect the arrow was amazing. You can do the same if they attack you."

She wanted to beg Grayson to come up with another plan, but she'd known before she'd brought him here that there was only one way to rescue Chenoa. "Don't call me and distract me. It might take a bit of time to convince him."

"Be careful."

She decided it was best not to tell him she planned to arrive as close to Skah as possible. She was counting on the surprise factor to give her a few seconds to tell him Chenoa needed him. "Call me if Lonan returns. I'll come straight back and get you out of here." She leaned close to kiss him before drawing back and dropping a flower to the ground. "You be careful too." She stepped on the flower, bringing to mind the image of Skah, his pure white feathers and rounded face.

Skah stepped forward at the same time as Summer arrived, an expression of shock momentarily crossing his face. "Guards!"

She drew back from him, sending a blast of air towards the door, slamming it shut so no one could enter. "Chenoa needs your help."

Skah drew a sword, attacking. "You were the one who stole her."

Drawing her own blade she blocked his attack, feeling the force of it vibrate through her arms. Behind her the guards tried to force their way through the wind she kept pushing against the door. "Lonan tricked me. He's made it impossible for me to get close enough to rescue her. I told him how close I arrive to a person." She didn't tell him that had changed.

"Do you truly think I'm going to fall for your lies?"

"I can't lie. I have magic."

"A few little tricks." He attacked again. "More likely enchantments you've bought off someone else to throw around as needed."

She blocked, jumping back out of the way of his next attack. Was that possible? She thought of the crystal the doctor had given her to use. Maybe it was. "Let me show you. Give me two minutes to convince you. I don't know how long Chenoa has." She didn't know how long she could defend herself. Already her arms were weakening. "Two minutes. Please. I can't save her. What I tried nearly got her killed. There are traps."

"What kind of traps?"

She blocked his next blow, noticing it wasn't as strong as the previous ones had been. "Spikes, animal traps and arrows."

Skah stepped back, lowering his sword. "You have one minute."

She held up her hand, forcing magic to pool in it. "I have my own magic. It's why I had to help Lonan. I accidentally took most of his."

Skah laughed, a screeching sound to it. "I'd heard someone had stolen his magic. That's what made it easy to capture him." His expression hardened. "Then you had to set him free and help him steal my daughter."

She let the magic sink back into her hand, the sensation odd. "Let me take you to Chenoa. I can't get close enough to save her. Not without killing her and that's the last thing I want to do."

"What is the catch?"

"That you don't retaliate against Grayson or me or against anyone we care about. Or have someone retaliate on your behalf." She tried to think how Grayson had worded their bargain with Lonan. There were probably a lot of important points she'd missed. "We have to hurry. She was crying."

"Now I know you're lying. Chenoa wouldn't be crying because she was taken captive."

"It was after an arrow nearly went through her."

Skah sheathed his sword. "Take me to her."

She sheathed her own sword and took his hand, stepping to the side of him. "It's a narrow ledge." Dropping a flower on the floor, she stepped on it, the world going out of focus as the door was driven open and Raptors poured into the room a second before they left. They arrived on the ledge next to Grayson and Summer let go of Skah's hand.

The Raptor flew into the air, aiming straight for his daughter who was frantically shaking her head again. Skah circled around the area where she was being held captive.

Grayson reached for Summer's hand. "What happened?"

"I'll tell you about it later."

Skah returned to them, dropping onto the ledge beside Summer. "You didn't tell me about all the fine lines he's used to create another layer of traps."

"What lines?"

"Around Chenoa. He anticipated Raptors helping too. The only way to her is from above, but my wings are too wide to land safely. If we had rope I could lower you through the gap."

She eyed the distance between Chenoa's head and the ground she stood on. The Raptor wasn't too tall.

"No," Grayson said. "Don't think about it. There could be pressure points where she's standing and you'll both be shot."

"What are you considering doing?" Skah demanded.

Summer looked from Grayson to Chenoa and back to Grayson. "We might have been tricked, but it's partly my fault. I was the one who accidentally took his magic. He wouldn't have been captured if I hadn't done that."

"You'll get yourself killed," Grayson said.

She wanted to disagree, but the words wouldn't come. Obviously she feared it was a possibility too. "We can't leave her there."

Grayson sighed heavily. "Be careful."

"As much as possible." She turned to Skah who'd watched their exchange. "Lower me as much as you can then give me a ten second warning before you let go."

"How will you lower yourself the rest of the way?"

"With magic." It was more than that, but it was the easiest explanation she could make without lying about it.

"If you survive and my daughter doesn't, it won't be for long. She needs to be saved for our pact to be binding." Skah lifted her up, flying towards Chenoa.

She'd expected Skah would retaliate if something went wrong. She'd have preferred it if he hadn't confirmed it. At least not until everything was over. Seeing her destination was coming closer, she gathered wind towards her feet, ready to use it to slow her descent. When Skah gave her a ten second warning, she struggled to make the air solid beneath her feet. He let go and she dropped faster than she'd expected, struggling to draw in more air to slow her progress.

Chenoa shook her head frantically as Summer continued to lower herself, reaching out to pull the gag down. It was a lot harder to do than she'd expected with how tightly it had been tied.

"Don't touch the ground." Chenoa's words tumbled over themselves. "It'll kill both of us."

Summer tried to keep the air beneath her feet as she drew her sword and used it to cut away the ropes that kept Chenoa in place. She sheathed her sword the moment she was finished. "Raise your arms." She wrapped her arms around the woman before calling out, "Pull us out of here."

Skah flew in and grabbed Chenoa's hands, pulling both of them upwards.

"Arrows!" Grayson shouted the word.

Chapter Twenty-Five

She heard countless arrows coming towards them, cutting through the air. She hadn't released the breeze from beneath her feet. Holding tighter to Chenoa, she forced the breeze to swirl around the three of them, dragging more air in towards them.

Most of the arrows were deflected, a few of them got through, doing only minor damage. They reached the ledge where Grayson stood calling out Summer's name. Skah dropped the two of them, landing as well.

Grayson wiped at the blood on Summer's arms and legs, the arrows having sliced into her clothes. "How badly are you hurt? Are any of them deep?"

She brushed away his hands. "Mostly scratches."

"Mostly? What about the rest of them?"

She didn't bother answering. There was no way

she could lie. A few of them probably needed stitches. She turned to Chenoa. "Are you okay?"

Skah knelt in front of his daughter, his wings flowing down his back like a cloak, his eyes flashing with anger. "He broke her wings." His gaze met Summer's. "He's dead. Next time I see Lonan I'll kill him."

She didn't doubt him at all. "I have no ties to him."

"Good. If you stand between us you will die too."

"Will her wings heal?" Grayson asked.

Skah nodded. "In time." He pointed a finger at Summer. "You will return her home. I'll bring the boy. If you want him back you better be waiting there when we arrive." Skah scooped up Grayson, flying low through the cave towards the exit.

Summer turned to Chenoa, holding out her hand, a flower forming in her other one. "Are you ready to go?"

Chenoa placed a hand in hers. "Thank you for coming after me."

"I'm sorry I let him get you in the first place." She took them to the courtyard where Lonan had stolen Chenoa, arriving near the raised pond. It was the only place other than the dungeon that she could visualise clearly enough. Raptors descended on them the moment they arrived and Summer swayed on her feet as Chenoa told them not to harm her.

By the time Skah returned with Grayson, Summer and Chenoa had been doctored, washed and changed into fresh clothes. She'd been right and a couple of the wounds had needed stitches. Her clothes hadn't been salvageable and Chenoa had promised that another set would be made for her, the same as the ones that had been ruined while rescuing her. For now, she wore a pair of black trousers and a brown shirt that had been borrowed from a human servant. She sat with Chenoa who talked about the many problems she'd had trying to make Lonan understand she wasn't interested in him. The Raptor hadn't believed Chenoa.

Grayson strode towards Summer, taking her hands and looking her over when she rose from the seat. Skah remained in the doorway of the room.

Summer drew a hand from Grayson's and pressed her fingers to his lips. "I'll live. Stop worrying."

"I haven't said anything."

She smiled. It had been in his eyes. "Are you ready to go home?" Not that she knew how she was going to take them anywhere with how exhausted she felt.

Before Grayson could speak, Skah strode into the room. "What do you want for saving my daughter?"

Summer shook her head. "We had to save her." She couldn't have lived with the guilt if she hadn't at least tried.

"As you said, you were tricked. Not everyone would have been as honourable as you and resolved the matter. I owe you for the life of my daughter. The traps were set not only for you, but also for me."

"We have a cottage that needs repairing," Grayson said.

"Done."

"It's nearly falling down," Summer said.

Skah waved a hand regally, as if brushing aside her concerns. "A small price compared to what Chenoa's life is worth."

"We'd prefer that no one knew where the cottage is," Grayson said.

Skah laughed. "I can see how that might be important considering how quickly you gain enemies. Lonan will not be pleased that you had a hand in taking Chenoa away from him."

Summer shared a look with Grayson, neither of them mentioning that Lonan couldn't retaliate. For any reason.

Skah continued speaking. "You can take workers and their supplies to your cottage or make other arrangements. The details can be sorted later. For now, I would like to offer you the hospitality of my home."

Relief rushed through Summer. There was no way she could have taken them anywhere else today. "Thank you."

"Anything you need, you have only to ask."

"Something to eat would be good," Grayson said.

Skah nodded, beckoning forward a servant who stood off to one side. "Organise it." The servant hurried away.

The meal was far more elaborate than any Summer had eaten. Afterwards, Skah presented Grayson with a sword, telling him he'd need it to protect himself from Lonan. Neither of them argued the matter and Grayson thanked Skah, strapping it on.

When it came time to retire, they were shown to an elaborate suite and Summer stood at the window, looking out over the canyon. "I feel like royalty." Her stomach slowly turned, but she could control the fear she normally felt when looking down from such a height.

Grayson came to stand behind her, wrapping his arms around her. "Our cottage will seem ordinary in comparison."

She turned in his arms, sliding hers around his neck

and smiling up at him. "The human world will seem ordinary in comparison."

"Does that mean we'll return?"

"We'll always return, but I don't know if I could live here permanently."

"That's a start." His lips met hers and his arms tightened around her. After several minutes, he drew back to meet her gaze. "We'll return to the human world tomorrow."

"You sure there isn't just one more thing we have to do?"

Grayson chuckled. "Actually, there is." He lowered his head and kissed her again.

Chapter Twenty-Six

The next morning Skah made sure Summer and Grayson were well fed before they left, giving them a calico sack each, telling them they were gifts to be opened later. They returned to their place after promising to visit again in the future, Chenoa the most insistent.

Summer stared at the cottage, smiling wryly. "A long way from castles and fancy suites."

Grayson slid his arm around her waist and drew her close. "This place will improve. Skah will make sure of it."

Summer looked down at the calico sack she held. "I wonder what he gave us." It felt mostly soft. "Do you think it's clothes?"

"Only one way to find out." Grayson headed for the front door, his arm remaining around her so that she walked with him. He dropped his arm and let her go ahead, remaining in the doorway. "There's not really anywhere clean to open it."

Summer formed a breeze to blow the dust and dirt off the table. It wasn't much cleaner.

"Dry it once I'm finished." Grayson moved closer to the table, water forming on the timber before rushing back and forth across the surface, swooping out the back door, black in colour.

Summer sent a breeze across the table, drying the surface. She grinned. "That worked well. But I hope you're not expecting us to clean the rest of the place that way. I think it's going to take a lot more than water and wind to get it in shape."

Grayson set the calico bag on the table and opened it up, taking out clothes to lay them on top of the bag. There was a gold edged card with them. After looking at the card, Grayson turned to Summer. "You better check what's in your bag."

She did the same, removing clothes that looked out of place in the ramshackle cottage. "Have we been invited to a party?" She reached for the gold edged card, staring at the fancy writing. 'We would like to offer you the position of honorary knight of our court. Entitled to our protection with no obligations on your behalf.' She turned to Grayson, holding out the card. "Does yours say the same?"

"Yeah."

"What are we going to tell Skah?"

"Yes?"

"But…" She tried to form a complete sentence. She failed.

"What's wrong?"

She slowly shook her head. "I'm no knight."

"They're the warriors and protectors of a land. After what you did for Oliver and Chenoa I'd say you are."

"Oliver is my brother. Of course I had to rescue him."

"And Chenoa?"

"I felt responsible. I don't want to feel responsible for an entire land."

"You won't need to. Skah wrote that we'd have no other obligations."

She stared at the words, thinking back over her conversations with the Raptor. "He thinks we'll feel obligated. He believes we have honour." She told him what Skah had said when she'd gone to him begging for help to rescue Chenoa.

"Is that so bad?"

"I don't know."

"We don't have to decide right away. We'll find

someone to take a message to him. Let him know we need to think about his offer."

"Okay." She put the clothes back in the bag. "Where are we going to leave them?" She looked down at herself. "And the ones we're wearing. We should wear our old clothes home. Last time I'd planned to change in the passageways and leave the clothes from here to collect later. I don't want to do that this time. These ones belong here for the times we return."

Grayson grinned. "The root cellar." He paused a moment. "Will those times be visits or something more permanent?"

She shrugged. "I guess we'll have to wait and see."

It took them nearly half an hour to change into the clothes they'd worn the first day they'd arrived in the realms of the Fae. The drawstring bag of clothes had been by the front door where Summer had dropped them after Grayson had been captured. They left the rest of their gear in the root cellar. Summer hadn't wanted to leave her sword behind.

"What if someone steals it?" She clasped her hands together in an effort not to pick it up again.

"Then we'll track them down and take it back."

Unclasping her hands, she pointed a finger at him. "Get that look out of your eyes."

"What look?"

She slowly shook her head. "You know exactly what one I'm talking about." She followed him out of the root cellar, wanting to run back and grab her sword. "Maybe we should buy a padlock for the root cellar."

Grayson grinned, a familiar expression in his eyes. "Is that a yes to something more permanent?"

"Your sword is down there too," Summer said. "It isn't only mine."

He stepped close. "I'll sort something out. Don't worry. Your gear will be here when you return for it."

She pressed a hand against his chest when he tried to come closer. "We need to go home before something else happens."

"I'm ready whenever you are."

She looked down at herself. There were scrapes, cuts, stitches and bruises visible on her arms and legs. Her clothes were permanently stained from climbing through the tunnels, even though they'd been cleaned, and they were ripped and torn in places. Her parents were going to be full of questions. Ones she couldn't answer. Opening her hand, she held up a strawberry flower. "I'm as ready as I'm likely to be."

"Take us to the blacksmith. There's a tavern not

far from there. We can find someone who can take a message to Skah for us." He took her hand.

She let the flower drift to the ground, staring at it a moment before she stepped on it and took them to the blacksmith at the courtyard markets. After greeting him and confirming that the rumours were true and they had helped rescue Chenoa, they headed for the tavern. It didn't take long to buy a piece of paper, a thick creamy parchment, and write a message for Skah.

Grayson handed over one of the coins, that the doctor had given them, to the bartender who promised to see the letter was delivered. He slid his arm around Summer's waist once they stepped outside, walking towards the alley and the tunnel that led them to the human world.

Before they could enter the narrower alleys Lonan dropped down out of the sky and landed in front of them. Summer reached for a sword that wasn't there. "What do you want, Lonan?"

"You stole Chenoa." Lonan's hand rested on the hilt of the sword he wore.

Summer was tempted to ask him if he missed the one she'd taken. "You tricked us into helping you kidnap her. She doesn't love you."

"You better help me get her back," Lonan warned.

"Or what?" Grayson asked.

Lonan glared at them, not saying a word.

"You can't come after us for any reason. You made that deal," Summer said.

"You are the ones who tricked me." Lonan's hand remained on his sword.

Grayson half shrugged, smiling. "Then I guess we're even."

"We are not even. One day I'll figure out a loophole in the bargain we made and then you will regret crossing me."

Summer strode forward, stopping centimetres from Lonan. "That goes both ways. Cross us and you'll regret it." She didn't tolerate bullies in the human world. She wasn't going to tolerate them here.

"Think you can take me on?"

She stared at Lonan's expression, trying to figure out what it meant. She was pretty certain there was trickery involved.

Grayson chuckled. "I guess we'll never find out since our deal was bound with magic and there's no way out of it."

Lonan went back to glaring. "I will figure a way out eventually." He shot into the sky, wind rushing upwards with him, his wings stretching out once he was above the height of the buildings.

"He was trying to trick us into breaking the bargain, wasn't he?"

Grayson nodded. "Goading us into it."

She was starting to get the hang of this. Somehow she'd faced the impossible in the realms of the Fae and not only survived, but also triumphed. She grinned, surprised by how good that felt. "Let's go home and let our family know we're alive."

Grayson grinned. "Then we can work on returning here permanently."

"We'll see."

They walked to the tunnel, side-by-side, Summer looking around the alleys they walked through. She was surprised by the sense of sadness she felt at leaving. At least she'd figured out that much. She'd miss this place enough that she'd want to visit.

Summer climbed through the tunnel first, a breeze rushing over her. She was surprised to find it was late afternoon, the passage dimly lit from the light filtering down from above, the temperature hot. She guessed it was summer. Hopefully the same year they'd left.

Grayson came through the tunnel and stood beside her. "Need a bucket of water to cope with the heat?"

She laughed at the look in his eyes. "Don't even think about it."

"Grayson?"

They both turned in the direction of the voice, Grayson heading towards it. "Frank? What are you doing here?"

"My turn to watch for you."

Summer stopped in front of the man who towered over her, about an inch taller than Grayson. "What day is it? Are my family okay?"

"You missed Christmas. Spencer was sure you'd be back in time for Christmas. He was going to call you, but didn't want to distract you in case you were dealing with major trouble." Frank led the way through the passageways in the cliff.

"What day is it?" Summer asked again.

"Twenty-eighth of December."

Chapter Twenty-Seven

Summer stared at Frank's back as he kept walking. Two months until she was eighteen. Sixteen days since she'd learned about the existence of the Fae. Which was odd since only a week had passed for her. "You didn't say if my family are okay."

Frank glanced over his shoulder. "Worried. Beginning to think they'll never see you again."

"Oh."

"What are you going to tell them?" Frank asked.

"The truth," Grayson said.

"Spencer said you had Fae magic. Thought he must have been joking. But I guess you've been saying for years that you'd get some." Frank glanced over his shoulder again. "You two are screwed. There's no way you can lie about where you were and there's no way they'll believe the truth."

"The truth is we can't tell them anything," Grayson said.

Frank chuckled. "I guess that'll do. If you can manage to keep telling them that."

"We'll have to," Grayson said.

"We don't have a choice," Summer said.

"Both of you have magic?" Frank stepped out of the cliff's ravine and turned to face them.

Summer nodded.

"You going back with him when he goes?"

She shrugged.

"You do know it's not safe back there."

She couldn't help laughing, glancing towards Grayson. "So I've been told." She slipped her hand in Grayson's. "What are you going to tell them about finding us?"

"That none of us gave up searching. Those of us with a license took turns coming out here every day. Even on Christmas day. The adults kept telling us we were wasting our time. Whoever took you had probably taken you both a long way from here."

Grayson clapped Frank on the shoulder. "Thanks."

"Ready to face everyone?"

Summer thought of Kimberley and was tempted to say no. She remained silent, walking between Grayson and Frank. When they reached the car, both her and Grayson stepped back. "I didn't think about that. We should have got rid of the excess magic before we returned."

Grayson sighed. "It's not too bad for me, what about you?"

"I've got an empty juice bottle in the car," Frank said.

"Glass?" Grayson asked.

Frank nodded, opening up the front door and reaching in to get it. "It'll need washing."

"That's not a problem." Grayson took the bottle and opened the lid, water filling the bottom within seconds. He tipped it out and filled it several more times before handing it over to Summer to dry.

By the time the two of them had drained off their excess magic, the bottle was a third full, most of the magic from Summer. She stared at the bottle. "What are we going to do with it?"

Frank held out his hand. "I can look after it until it's safe for you to have it."

Grayson nodded. "Thanks."

Summer handed the bottle to Frank, who put it in the glove box, locking it. She could now get in the car, finding it only mildly uncomfortable. How was she meant to live in a world filled with iron? For a moment she could only think it was impossible.

Straightening her shoulders and lifting her head, she stared out the window. If this was the world she wanted to live in, she'd figure out a way to stay.

It was a long drive back to town and Summer had plenty of time to worry about what her family were going to say. They pulled up at Grayson's family's place first. His mother opened the door and stared at the two of them like they were ghosts.

"Grayson?" His mother pulled him close, tears falling silently down her face.

Summer stood in the doorway, feeling awkward.

Spencer came running, grinning. "What took you so long?"

Grayson pulled away from his mother to hug his brother, slapping him on the back. "How did it feel to do my chores for a change?"

Spencer laughed. "Should have known that's why you stayed away so long."

"We have to ring Summer's parents," Grayson's mother said.

"I can take her over to the place they're staying at," Frank offered.

In the end, Grayson went with Frank and Summer, his mother having argued about remaining behind. Frank had pointed out that Summer's family didn't need an audience and that she should call to let them know Summer was on the way. When they arrived, it was to find the police were there too and her mum wanted to take her to the hospital. She refused, wishing she hadn't when the police continued to question them. Kimberley arrived part way through the questioning and when she made her usual complaints about Summer, was politely sent from the room by the police. Her interruption didn't make a difference. The questioning continued.

Summer clung to Grayson's hand as she kept saying she couldn't tell anyone anything. At one stage they were separated and she was asked if it was Grayson she feared.

She stared at the police officer that sat across the table from her. "No. I'd never fear Grayson. I might fear for him, but I'm not afraid of him. Grayson would never hurt me."

"Then why can't you tell us what happened to you. Or where you were."

"I can't." She took Grayson's stone from her pocket, rubbing her fingers across the smooth surface before holding it loosely and resting her chin on her hand in the hope Grayson would be able to hear her. "There are some things I can tell you. There were times when it was dark and we were in a tunnel. Sometimes I thought there were monsters. Do you know how hard it is to tell what's around you in the dark?"

"How did you get away?"

"There's not much I can tell you. Do you think I can see in the dark?"

"Were you kept in the dark all the time?"

"Please. I can't answer any more questions. I'm tired." Tired of the questioning and fatigued from all the iron.

"Whoever took the three of you could be out there kidnapping someone else. Look at the state you returned home in. Do you want someone else to go through what you've been through?" the Officer asked.

She thought of the times she'd passed out. "There were times I was unconscious. I can't tell you everything that happened while I was gone because I don't know all of it."

The officer kept her gaze on Summer.

She returned the stare, refusing to look away. No one believed in the Fae and showing them she could do magic would probably only lead to other problems. "Are we finished?" She rose to her feet before the officer could reply.

"When you've had time to think things over we'll talk again." The officer stood, her voice stern.

Summer couldn't make the sarcastic reply she wished to make. Her magic obviously didn't take into account sarcasm. It saw it as a lie. "Does that mean we can't go back home yet? I want to get on with my life."

"I'm sure you'd like to put all of this behind you, but until whoever kidnapped you is found, then you'll never truly get past this."

She wanted to tell the officer how wrong she was. All she could do was remain silent.

"Call me the moment you remember anything." The officer held out a card.

Summer took it, leaving the room. Grayson was in the hallway and she went into his arms, wrapping her arms around him, continuing to clutch the stone. She hadn't realised it'd be so difficult. Hadn't realised she'd have to talk to the police.

"Summer?"

She turned in Grayson's arms to face her mum.

"They said you wouldn't tell them anything." Julie looked to Grayson. "Either of you."

"What does Oliver remember?" Grayson asked.

"A cage and a strange looking man. One he wasn't able to describe."

"Why would you think we could remember any more than he was able to?" Grayson asked.

Summer stared at her mum, who remained silent, her eyes filled with unshed tears. The silence stretched out and she began to feel uncomfortable. "I'm hungry."

"Were you fed while you were gone?"

"Sometimes. Not every meal," Summer said.

"I'll get you something to eat."

Summer leaned back against Grayson as she watched her mum walk away. When they were alone, she slipped the stone back into her pocket as she turned to him, moving close so she could whisper in his ear. "What are we going to do?"

"We'll figure it out. The comments you made to the policewoman were good. Eventually they'll stop asking questions and accept that we can't answer them."

"I can't spend day after day being questioned like this."

"You won't." Grayson paused a moment. "There is another option."

"I'm not running away either. If we return, it won't be because we're escaping. It'll be because we want to and we will return to see our families." She couldn't help thinking about the doctor whose family had aged without him.

"One day you won't be able to."

"What about a glamour?"

"Where did you hear about that?"

"From the boy with the map. Could it be used to make us look older?"

"Yeah."

Behind them the front door opened and they both spun to face it, Summer's hand going for a sword she didn't have with her.

"Summer!" Oliver ran towards her, Tim frozen in the doorway. Oliver threw his arms around her.

She bent to hug him back. "Are you okay?"

"Aunt Kimberley kept saying you wouldn't be back."

"Of course I came back."

"She said you wouldn't be able to come home because you were dead."

At a sound, Summer looked past her brother to her stepdad. She'd never seen him look so angry before. She watched as he strode past them, Oliver continuing to ramble on. A few minutes later they heard raised voices. Tim and Kimberley.

"Why don't we go outside?" Grayson asked.

"Good idea." Summer took hold of her brother's hand. "It'll be nice outside."

Once they were all sitting on the footpath, Oliver asked, "Do you remember a cage too?"

"Yes." She'd hated leaving him in it.

"They keep asking me questions, but I can't remember anything. Or at least not much. Do you have that problem too?"

She nodded, unable to say yes.

"I'm glad it's not just me."

She draped an arm around her brother's shoulders. "You're safe now."

They fell silent, none of them talking until Julie came outside to call them in to eat. The meal was silent, but not in a companionable way. It felt awkward and Kimberley spent most of the time glaring at Tim and Summer.

The next couple of days continued like the first day they'd returned. Grayson spent every minute possible with Summer, sneaking back after he'd supposedly gone home for the night. When Julie said it was time for them to return home, Summer started to protest.

Grayson took her hand, squeezing it. "I was thinking of visiting the coast."

Hearing the question in his tone, she met his gaze. "Yes."

"I'll meet you down there. I need to take a bit of a detour on the way."

"Where to?"

"Visit Skah."

She wanted to ask him what he planned, but that would have to wait until later. When they were alone. She also wanted to tell him to use the portals until he was better at magic. That too would have to wait until later.

It was a lot later than she'd expected. Her mum had tried to lecture her on having time away from Grayson so she could see their relationship had only developed because of what they'd suffered together. Unable to explain why she knew it wasn't, Summer remained silent. Her magic didn't allow her to lie, not even to herself. She thought of the day, so long ago, when she'd first met Grayson. When she was twelve and he was thirteen. The expression in his eyes had intrigued her even then.

"Are you listening, Summer?"

She nodded.

"We've arranged for you to talk to someone when we return home. You never used to be so quiet or staring off into space all the time."

Summer stood up. "If that is all, I might get ready for bed." Being able to only tell the truth made it hard to talk when there was so much to hide.

Julie sighed, reaching out to hug Summer. "We were terrified we'd never see you again."

"I know." She held onto her mum for a moment

before retreating to her room, waiting for Grayson to sneak in so she could question him. By the time he arrived, it was late and questions were soon forgotten.

Chapter Twenty-Eight

Summer tried to get back into her normal routine when they returned home, but it was difficult since school holidays didn't have a routine. And with school completely finished she couldn't expect the return of her normal routine. She'd planned to get a job and take a year off before starting university the following year. Now none of it seemed right.

Grayson spent the weekends with her, the weekdays he spent in the realms of the Fae, having used the bottle of magic to increase his magic so he could travel more easily between the two realms. She called him, with the stone, every Friday night to let him know what time it was. Time didn't run the same in both realms. Her mum kept reminding her that their relationship wouldn't last and each time she had to stop herself from telling her mum why she was wrong.

Sunday night when Grayson left, he took with him a bottle of magic. Initially he'd been surprised at how quickly it regenerated. He'd asked Skah, who'd explained that Raptors tended to regenerate magic quicker than many other Demi Fae. The Raptor also waited for an answer from both of them. As yet Summer couldn't decide what to tell him

The first evening Summer returned to sword fighting the instructor took her aside. "You might want to sit this session out."

"Why?"

"This isn't the place to take your problems out on other people."

"I wasn't doing that."

"Then what were you doing?"

She opened her mouth to reply. Closing it again she shrugged. She'd been fighting for her life, not to score points.

"Take a seat." The instructor gestured towards the seats before he returned to the rest of the class.

She watched them, playing at fighting, none of it real. Sheathing her sword, she removed her gloves as she walked outside. It was dark, yet that wasn't a problem for her these days. The problem was that she felt like nothing was real. Everything was a game and didn't truly matter.

Her hand went to the hilt of her sword. Even it was a game, a toy. Not like the one she'd left behind in the root cellar. She took out her phone to check the time, sighing when she saw the battery was nearly flat. It never lasted these days. Nothing battery powered lasted when it was around her.

She turned on the voice recording app. "This isn't home anymore. Home is another place, another time. One where the stakes are real and nothing is a game. I'm not sure exactly where it is." She thought of the ramshackle cottage, Skah's castle and the Fringes. "But staying here isn't going to help me find it." Stopping the recording, she played it back, listening to herself speak the truth. The only thing she could speak these days.

Checking the time, she decided to walk home. It would be ages before Tim picked her up. She sent him a text to let him know he didn't need to collect her and strode down the street. On the way, she once more listened to the voice recording, the phone flashing a low battery warning as she reached the end.

Arriving home, she brushed aside Julie's questions and headed to her room, surveying it. There really wasn't much she needed, but she couldn't walk away with nothing. That would lead to questions she couldn't answer. Grabbing a cloth backpack, she threw in a change of clothes, a handful of gold jewellery, a couple of books and her favourite belt. The rest would be here if she wanted it later. She left her fake sword on the bed.

Once more she looked at the time before she placed the phone on her bedside drawers. Her gaze was drawn to the date. She'd been back twelve days. Why had she wasted so much time figuring it out? Tearing a piece of paper from a notebook, she wrote 'I'm sorry'. The words made her think of Grayson. Her lips curved into a smile and she drew out the stone. Being the weekend he'd spent the earlier part of the day with her, returning to the realms of the Fae while she was at sword training. She spoke against the surface, "I'm ready."

"I'll be there soon." His words hung in the air by her ear.

She returned her attention to the paper, not sure what to say. In the end, she wrote, 'I'll ring or email to let you know I'm okay.' She nearly crossed out the word ring. It'd be easier to write when there were so many things she couldn't say.

The smell of rain hung in the air and Grayson appeared in her room. He glanced at her bedside alarm clock. "You're finished early. What happened?" Picking up the piece of paper, he smiled as he read it.

"You're coming home with me?" He placed the note back on the bedside drawers.

"Yes."

"They'll be worried." He gestured towards the note.

"I know, but there isn't a lot I can tell them. It's better this way. They'll get used to me coming and going." She swung her backpack onto one shoulder.

"I need to visit the blacksmith before we go to our place. Do you want to take us there or should I?"

"You can. First, how many days have passed since I was last there."

"Four."

"Only four?"

Grayson grinned. "Yeah, only four. So don't go expecting a lot of miracles for our cottage." He held out his hand. "Are you ready?"

She placed her hand in his. "Yes." She'd been ready twelve days ago. It had taken her all this time to realise it.

Grayson dropped a raindrop shaped stone on the floor and stood on it, taking them to the blacksmith. The man grinned when he saw them, holding out a padlock and two keys. Grayson took them from him, examining the items.

"You're happy with them?" the blacksmith asked.

Grayson held one of the keys out to Summer. "Yes. Thanks. They're exactly what I wanted." He dropped some coins into the blacksmith's hand.

The blacksmith looked them over. "Why are neither of you wearing your swords?"

"People rarely wear swords when they visit the human realm," Grayson said.

"That's good. I thought the two of you might have given up on being fighters. There was someone asking around for help. Their father is missing. They heard how you'd rescued not one, but two people."

Summer smiled. Technically it was three since she'd also rescued Grayson at one stage. "Why would they want our help?"

"Because the two of you are honourable. Everyone has heard how you rescued Chenoa after being tricked by Lonan. It wasn't your fault, but you took responsibility anyway. You don't get much of that around here. What you do get are those looking out for themselves and far too many missing people. Ones that stumble on the secrets of others or hear too much. There's always someone willing to pay to have a loved one tracked down. The problem is that those who do the tracking can often be bought off by the ones who do the kidnapping."

Summer thought of how Lonan had tricked them

into thinking Chenoa loved him. "What about those who are trying to track down enemies?"

"You'd figure it out. After Lonan I'm sure you've learned a trick or two of your own. Think about it. It'd suit the pair of you."

"We'll think about it." She wasn't sure if they'd help. Look at all the problems they'd had going after Oliver and Chenoa.

Grayson slightly raised his hand that held the padlock. "Thank you for getting this done so quick." At the blacksmith's nod, he turned to Summer. "Ready to go home?" He held out a hand, palm up.

Those words sounded good to her. She placed her hand in his, the world shimmering then reforming. Laughter was surprised from her. "How did you trick me like that? You made it sound like not much had been done."

"Not a lot has been done. The roof no longer leaks and repairs have begun on the kitchen. It's a long way from completion." He held up the padlock. "Want to change your clothes and collect your sword before I lock the root cellar?"

She walked beside him around to the back of the cottage. "You've also done plenty of cleaning up outside."

"There's more to be done. A lot more." He stopped

at the door to the root cellar. "Your things are in the same place. I'll be inside the cottage when you're ready."

She headed into the root cellar, glancing around the dim interior. Everything looked the same down here. It didn't take her long to dress in the clothes Chenoa had given her. She held the sword she'd taken from Lonan, thinking back over everything that had happened. It had been resting near the sword Skah had given Grayson.

Picking up the second sword, she turned to head out of the root cellar. Grayson entered. She froze. "What's wrong?"

"I was worried when you took so long." He nodded towards the swords she held. "Is there a problem?"

She held his sword out to him, buckling her own on once he'd taken his. It felt right having it hanging at her side. A real weapon, not a toy. "I want to tell Skah yes."

Finished buckling on his weapon, Grayson looked over at her with a grin. "And the person who's missing their father?"

She met his gaze, seeing the familiar look of excitement, mischief and laughter. "Someone has to rescue him." This wasn't a game. Lives were at stake.

Grayson stepped close, his arms going around her. "And it might as well be someone who's honourable?"

She looked up at him, her arms going around his waist. "I'm not about to let it be someone who'd take the highest bid." An image came to mind of Chenoa on the ledge above the crocodiles. "That isn't right."

Grayson chuckled. "You've got that look in your eyes."

"What look?"

"The one you always accuse me of having."

She laughed. "Good. Because interesting things happen when you have that look in your eyes. Let's see how interesting they get now we both have it." She pressed her lips against his. This wasn't a game and she wasn't playing. She was ready to live.

Free Ebook

Subscribe to Avril's newsletter to receive a free ebook. This ebook is exclusive to those on her mailing list. To find out more about this offer visit: www.avrilsabine.com/free-ebook

*

We value your privacy and will not sell, rent, exchange or loan your email address to third parties. Your information is confidential and you are under no obligation to remain on the mailing list and can unsubscribe at any time.

Acknowledgements

Thanks to all my usual crew. I couldn't manage without you. And in particular Cat, thank you for helping me name this book.

To The Reader

If you enjoyed this book, why not consider leaving a review to help other readers discover it too? Reader engagement is one of the few ways that lets an author know readers want more books in a particular series or genre. So leave a review and tell friends, not only about this book but also about other ones you've enjoyed, so you can continue to enjoy books by your favourite authors for years to come.

Dreams are meant to be lived,

Avril.

About The Author

Avril is an Australian author who lives with her family on acreage in South East Queensland. She writes mostly young adult speculative fiction, but has been known to dabble in other genres. You can find more information about her at her website www.avrilsabine.com where you can also subscribe for her newsletter to be kept informed about new releases, current projects, blog posts and exclusive news.

Titles By Avril Sabine

Stories about strong characters and characters who discover their strengths.

SERIES

Assassins Of The Dead- Young Adult Fantasy/ Paranormal

Book 1: Dark Blade

Book 2: Dragon Touched

Book 3: Society Against Vampires

Book 4: King's Request

Dragon Blood- Young Adult Urban Fantasy (with elements of romance)

(5 book series)

Book 1: Pliethin

Book 2: Wyvern

Book 3: Surety

Book 4: Knight

Book 5: Mage

Dragon Mage- Young Adult Urban Fantasy (with elements of romance)

(Series two of Dragon Blood series)

Book 1: Promise

Dragon Blood Chronicles- Young Adult Urban Fantasy (with elements of romance)

(Companion stand alone series to Dragon Blood)

Book 1: Oath

Book 2: Betrayed

Guardians Of The Round Table- Young Adult Fantasy LitRPG

(Co-written with Storm and Rhys Petersen)

Book 1: Dexterity Fail

Book 2: Goblin Boots

Book 3: Singed Feathers

Book 4: Frog Mage

Book 5: Crystal Mine

Book 6: Cursed Harp

Rosie's Rangers- Young Adult Western Steampunk

(6 book series)

Book 1: Justice

Book 2: Vengeance

Book 3: Treachery

Book 4: Accused

Book 5: Wanted

Book 6: Corruption

Mark Of Kings- Children's Fantasy

(Upper middle grade/preteen)

(4 book series)

Book 1: The Arena

Book 2: The Island

Book 3: The Assassin

Book 4: The King

Mark Of Kings- Children's Fantasy

(Upper middle grade/preteen)

(4 book series)

Book 1: The Arena

Book 2: The Island

Book 3: The Assassin

Book 4: The King

STAND ALONE SERIES

Demon Hunters- Young Adult Urban Fantasy/ Horror (with elements of romance)

Book 1: Blood Sacrifice

Book 2: Retribution

Book 3: Tainted

Book 4: Premonition

Book 5: Cursed

Book 6: Feud

Book 7: Extrication

Plea Of The Damned- Young Adult Urban Fantasy/Paranormal

(6 book series)

Book 1: Forgive Me Lucy

Book 2: Forgive Me Aiden

Book 3: Forgive Me Jena

Book 4: Forgive Me Kobe

Book 5: Forgive Me Marti

Book 6: Forgive Me Dawson

Realms Of The Fae- Young Adult Urban Fantasy (with elements of romance)

The Sword (short story in Like A Girl Anthology)

Heart Of Stone

Book 1: A Debt Owed

Book 2: Marked By The Hunt

Book 3: The Magic Collector

Book 4: An Unexpected Betrayal

Book 5: Imprisoned By Iron

Fairytales Retold (Short Stories)

Snow-White And Rose-Red

The Twelve Brothers

The Light Princess

Beauty And The Beast

Sleeping Beauty

Aschenputtel

The Golden Bird

The Frog Prince

The Death Of Koshchei The Deathless

Myths And Legends Retold (Short Stories)

Ion, Son Of Apollo

Sir Gawain And The Maid With The Narrow Sleeves

Princess Ilse, The Giant's Daughter

YOUNG ADULT NOVELS

Young Adult Fantasy (with elements of romance)

Elf Sight

Earth Bound

Young Adult Urban Fantasy

Stone Warrior (with elements of romance)

The Jungle Inside

Young Adult Contemporary (with elements of romance)

Through Your Eyes

The Ugly Stepsister

Perfect Little Princess

Young Adult Contemporary/Paranormal

Whispers In The Dark (with elements of romance and same sex relationships)

Over Too Soon (with elements of romance)

Young Adult Sci-Fi

Experiment X-One-Six (Urban Sci-Fi/Superheroes)

An Endless Dawn (Post Apocalyptic Sci-Fi)

CHILDREN'S BOOKS

Dragon Lord (Preteen/early teens) (Fantasy)

The Irish Wizard (Upper middle grade) (Urban Fantasy)

SHORT STORIES

Urban Fantasy

Eternally Late

Dealings With Joe

Glimpses (short story in That Moment When Anthology)

Contemporary

The Brat Next Door

Fantasy LitRPG

(Set in the same world as Guardians Of The Round Table Series)

Tales Of Inadon 1: The Disc (Co-written with Storm and Rhys Petersen) (short story in Game On! Anthology)

Post Apocalyptic Sci-Fi

Compulsive Directive

NONFICTION

A Year Of Weekly Writing Exercises (Creative Writing)

Cooking For Families With Allergies (Cooking) (Co-written with Storm Petersen)

Tell Me A Story, Grandma (Memoir)

For the most up to date details on available titles visit:

www.avrilsabine.com/books/bibliography

Realms Of The Fae Series

To learn more about this series visit:

www.avrilsabine.com/series/rotf

BOOKS AVAILABLE IN THE REALMS OF THE FAE SERIES

The Sword (short story in Like A Girl Anthology)

Heart Of Stone

Book 1: A Debt Owed

Book 2: Marked By The Hunt

Book 3: The Magic Collector

Book 4: An Unexpected Betrayal

Book 5: Imprisoned By Iron

Disclaimer

This is a work of fiction. Names, characters, businesses, places, events and incidents are either the products of the author's imagination or used in a fictitious manner. Any resemblance to actual persons, living or dead, or actual events is purely coincidental.

www.ingramcontent.com/pod-product-compliance
Lightning Source LLC
Chambersburg PA
CBHW050757190726
48285CB00005B/1695